I0535644

Breaking Waves
(Rebuilding Janey Holland)

by

Anthony Ashpitel

ANTHONY ASHPITEL

ISBN 978-0-9569003-0-2

Published by Anthony Ashpitel
Email: tonyashpitel@btinternet.com

Re-worked from film script to novel 2011

This book is dedicated to my wife, Anne, who is a boundless source of help and encouragement.

AA

As a writer I am a little out of my comfort zone with 'Breaking Waves'. It responds to my wife's request for her to proof-read something other than a succession of thriller type novels. By taking up the challenge, I hope to prove I have a feminine side, something my wife disputes.

AA

A trawl of the internet reveals general agreement on the symptoms which could trigger a psychotic episode, what used to be known as a 'nervous breakdown'. Although the full range of such symptoms is listed below, not all will be present in an individual heading for such an event.

- Disinterest in work or family life.
- Disinterest in social life or alienation from previously close friends and family.
- Sleep disruption or much longer periods of sleep.
- Significant changes in appetite, such as eating too little or too much.
- Paranoid thoughts, such as the thought that people are trying to harm you.
- Thoughts of invincibility.
- Persistent feelings of anxiety or panic attacks.
- Hearing voices.
- Seeing people who are not there.
- Thoughts of dying or wishing to die.
- Exhibiting strong or violent anger.
- Increasing dependence on alcohol or drugs.
- Inability to pursue a normal life, normal activities or normal relationships.
- Having flashbacks to a prior traumatic event

Prologue

The tiny disc ricocheted off the walls of the landing with a noise not unlike that of the ball kicking against the obstructions of a slowing roulette wheel. Then it continued to spin down in place with only the merest noise as it came to a stop on the hardwood floor at the foot of the ladder. Above, a dim illumination penetrated the black square of the open hatch and lit the underside of the roof in a soft glow.

Once the disc had come to rest it revealed itself as a plastic button. It had arrived at its resting place through the loft access. Now a shadow fell across it and the ladder as a figure placed a tentative foot on the bottom rung.

Sat atop a pile of old suitcases, Janey clasped her knees tightly to her chest so that the long nightdress draped down over her feet. Over this garment she wore a woollen cardigan, now missing a button, wrenched off and sent flying moments before. In this position she rocked slowly, backwards and forwards, all the time whimpering softly. She appeared to be in a sort of trance.

In front of her, no more than five feet away in the dimness was the bright square of light that was the loft access. As she stared in its general direction a shadow grew larger against the roof joists above her head.

Sat at the desk in his study, Doctor Cardle leant forward to the computer keyboard and began typing: 'I suppose there are many milestones on the way to a nervous breakdown,' he wrote. 'Each is marked by an increasing inability to cope; sometimes with even trivial levels of stress. If detected early the sufferer can usually help themselves to a full recovery without the need for drugs or therapy. A few days off or a holiday should do the trick.'

He reached out for a brandy glass placed close to his laptop and took a sip. He savoured the liquid before swallowing – as he always did - but he was going through the motions, his mind miles away. Then he turned back once again to the computer and continued to type. 'A complete nervous breakdown is rare. Usually the sufferer or an outsider intervenes to prevent further harm either by removing the problem, or by teaching the person to cope. Of course, this presumes that the sufferer admits there is a problem in the first place….and there's the rub.'

The shadow on the underside of the roof grew larger in the light cast through the loft access. As it did so, the ladder creaked slightly.

Janey, still sat atop the suitcases, appeared not to notice any of this. She noticed very little as she continue to mewl and rock back and forth. Even when the head of a child appeared through the hatch, followed quickly by her body, Janey seemed not to see her.

'Mummy!' called the child.

Janey did not respond and the child moved towards her and reached up, arms outstretched. Slowly, Janey lowered her knees and brought her arms around the child, all the while continuing her whimpering and without altering her gaze.

Doctor Cardle was thoughtful for a moment as he sought the words to describe his painful tale. He picked up his drink again and swirled the spirit in the glass before taking another small sip. Then he leaned forward again to the keyboard.

'This is the story of Janey Holland. Serial offender,' he wrote. 'She's several miles along the road to her irreversible breakdown. Just about at the burn-out stage. You wouldn't particularly know it. She's both very good at hiding her problem - at least outside her home - and at not admitting she has a problem. Not even to herself.

'So it's up to someone else to help her. But how, if the person is in denial? Well, you need a plan and need to be patient. Of course there are risks with any plan. You have to be careful. Plans can go wrong, sometimes very wrong. Still, it's a chance you take, isn't it? Sometimes you need to take a chance, even if it means you will place them in danger and might lose the one person you ever loved right along with it...'

Chapter One

The clock on the wall showed 13:05 above the brightly lit office on the twelfth floor. It was a large room, having a conference table along one side and away from a large desk. On the walls were various boards displaying schematics on the activities of Janey's department. Another wall was dominated by a large picture, depicting cliffs and waves crashing against rocks. It was a good picture and the subject was clear even if the execution was poor.

Gathered around the conference table were four people. Janey was running the meeting as usual and was attended by one of her project managers and his assistant. Janey's PA, Claire, was taking the minutes.

Janey was not in the best of moods. She was stressed and was fighting to control herself. The subject of her wrath was Steve, the project manager with her in this meeting.

In her opinion, Steve was being difficult. 'I'm just saying we don't have sufficient data to form a judgement yet,' he whined.

Janey was exasperated. 'With a few million customers waiting for the system to come back up I'd suggest we can't wait for all the information to come in before we do something,' she said, sarcastically. 'We need to be pragmatic!'

Steve looked away and she broke off from glaring at him to look at the picture on the wall.

'Okay,' said Mike, Steve's assistant, upbeat and leaning forward, his tone business-like. 'The reboot failed on the CTI changes. We just post the message on the web site that the e-service is temporarily down and customers will have to use voice mail for their transactions.'

This got Janey's attention. 'How long?'

Before Mike could answer, Steve shot a look at him. In response, Mike looked away deferentially.

Then the phone rang and Claire went to her desk to answer it.

Mike tried again. 'The message will be displayed as soon as we reboot without the CTI interface enabled. We can be back up by three.'

The PA handed Janey the phone, mouthing the word silently: 'Martin'.

She winced but took the phone. 'Martin. Yes,' she answered, with a cheerfulness she did not feel.

In the *Launch Area* in the City offices of the major bank a number of screens were blinking above a panel of six people. Above them a banner proclaimed: 'Berkley - the service you deserve.' The expressions on the faces of the panel were several versions of embarrassment. In the centre of the line was an empty seat. To the right of this activity, in the shadows, Martin was using a mobile phone. A go-fer stood by his side, moving about nervously.

Martin looked at the crowd of people in front of the panel. A tic jerked at the side of his eye briefly and he turned away to concentrate on the phone call. 'What the hell is going on?' he whispered. 'Have you fixed it yet?'

'We've got a short-term solution,' responded Janey. 'It will mean clients have to revert to using the phone operators.'

'When do we get the back-up system in place?'

'Three.'

'And the system I'm supposed to be launching to-day?' There was no disguising the antagonism in his voice.

Janey sighed and rubbed her eyes. 'Hopefully by the time we reboot tonight.'

'Hopefully? That's bloody wonderful,' he hissed. 'Remind me to have *you* front the next one of these. I want it up and running by open doors tomorrow or you can find another job. Okay, get on with it. I've got some fast talking to do.'

Martin turned back to the room and smiled. The tic returned.

Back in her office, Janey put down the phone and turned to Steve. 'We need the quick fix in place ASAP.'

Steve turned and gave Mike an enquiring look.

Mike responded instantly: 'Use your phone?' Instead of waiting for a reply from Janey he went over to her desk, picked up the phone, and was soon talking quietly.

Janey was looking at Steve. 'We have until the daily reboot of the e-service to get the fix in and to bring the new features on line.'

'Tall order,' suggested Steve. 'We'll try.'

'Don't just try,' she snapped. 'Do it! I want a status report at three-thirty. I need to know before the HoDs meeting at four.'

Mike returned to his seat at the conference table. 'We're all set for the quick fix,' he announced.

'Thanks, Mike,' responded Janey. She turned to Steve. 'Three-thirty.'

At this Steve and Mike made to leave and Janey opened the door.

'Steve, will you wait a minute?' she asked.

As Steve turned around Janey glanced over to her PA, who picked up the familiar signal and left the room.

Janey closed the door and turned to Steve. 'I need a lot more support, Steve,' she began. 'We launched early on your say-so. I can deal with mistakes but when you lose interest and become surly well, it's bloody unhelpful to say the least.'

'It's not my fault,' he responded. 'There've been too many launches recently. We can't keep up.'

'This is a different tune to what you've been singing so far. You've always signed up to the launch plan.'

'There's too much change,' he retorted.

'Our job is to deal with change. Change is the norm.'

'But there is too much change to fit in.'

'It's tight, I know, but we have to respond to business pressures. Nothing has changed except your attitude,' she reasoned.

Steve shook his head unhappily and left the office.

The door closed behind him.

Janey leaned with her back against the door. Then she slumped her shoulders and closed her eyes. She was shaking. The tears came but she made no sound.

'What's wrong with you?' she pleaded to herself. 'You can handle this. This is normal.'

She was still standing there a couple of minutes later when the phone rang. With an effort she moved towards the desk, brushing tears from her eyes.

She picked up her phone.

'Keep them there,' she said, too quickly. 'I'll be out in a minute. Lunch seems to have gone out the window again. Could you get me a sandwich and fresh coffee, please?'

Janey put down the phone and hurriedly dug away in her bag for her make-up. In a minute-or-so she had effected deft repairs.

'Pull yourself together, old girl,' she said to herself. 'Look on the bright side. You've a full two and a half hours before they beat you up at the HoDs meeting.'

Chapter Two

Janey carried Sunny into her bedroom and put her into bed. There was no tenderness in her movement – it was simply a chore. She pulled the covers over her daughter's shoulders and then turned towards the door. She left the room without a backward glance.

Janey's bedroom was dark as she entered. Her husband, Luke, was snoring loudly as she slipped into bed, instantly turning her back to him. Her eyes remained open.

Luke was sat at the desk in his study the following morning. He had left the door open, his habit so that he could listen out for Sunny. Around him toys littered the floor and a pile of laundry lay in a heap next to an ironing board.

On his desk in front of him was a large screen laptop computer.

Luke was wearing a headset and microphone and was leaning back in his chair, feet on the desk, with his hands clasped behind his neck.

'Character. Marty,' he said. 'Dialogue. I'm going to kill you.' He paused for a moment before continuing. 'Character. Chrissie. Dialogue. You don't mean that.'

Luke reached out a hand to the pile of laundry and picked up the first item he touched, a pair of his wife's knickers.

'Action,' he said. 'Marty picked up a thong and stretched it. He began to wind the ends around his hands as he walked towards his wife. 'Character. Chrissie. Dialogue. Oh! He does!'

On the screen of the laptop his spoken words were appearing in print. 'Pause. A beat,' he continued. 'Character. Chrissie. Dialogue. Wait a goddamn minute. They're my best knickers! D'you have any idea how much they cost?'

Luke pressed a button on the line connecting his headset to the computer. He smiled, a satisfied expression on his face. 'Ahh. No substitute for quality,' he said, quietly.

Moments later he turned as Janey entered the room. She was dressed for work.

Luke took off his headset and pressed a button on the laptop. The screen went blank.

No words were exchanged. Instead, Janey went through to the kitchen and Luke followed her.

Luke watched closely as she busied herself. He was leaning against a work surface and continued to study Janey as she sat at the breakfast table. She was lethargic as she arranged her breakfast, not looking his way. His expression was odd, reflective, coolly interested.

'Who were you talking to?' Janey didn't look up to him as she spoke.

'Oh,' said Luke, abruptly snapping out of his reverie. 'I'm working on a new idea.'

'That imagination of yours. Another story. Hardly practical.'

Luke moved over to Janey. He was angry. 'Does everything have to be? You can talk. The least practical person on the planet. Who does everything around here?'

Janey stiffened briefly.

Luke frowned. He moved over to where she was sitting and gently massaged her shoulders.

When he spoke his tone was soft. 'You got up again last night. Making quite a habit of it, aren't we? Things really bad still?'

'Nothing I can't handle.'

'We've heard that before.'

Doctor Cardle moved with difficulty to the window and looked out on the tenemented town-houses of Rome. It had been a beautiful day, now fast changing to dusk. Even so, the golden rays did nothing to lift the heaviness he felt and he closed the shutters to block out the light.

Then he returned to his keyboard and continued typing: 'Janey Holland had always felt in charge of herself and everything around her. That didn't mean she was competent to do everything but she knew how everything could be done, usually by others. She had excellent social skills which translated very well into effective management skills. Some would say she was manipulative but she was not scheming; she

16

simply knew what made people tick and how to get what she wanted out of them. This was a skill she had honed since her schooldays. It was a hard won skill; she had failed to get her way countless times and thrown her share of tantrums at her disappointments along the way, but she had prevailed, refining her methods, so that, by the time she left university, she was almost the complete article: to some, a high-flyer; to others, a bitch.

'She was still an attractive woman. She scrubbed up well, all agreed. Perhaps being habitually dressed in business clothes she lacked a wider allure but she was slim and had good skin and didn't look her 38 years. Even the puffiness under the eyes wasn't beyond the remedy of a little make-up and her regular features meant that she was still pleasing, if not stunning, to the eye.

'She had married late by modern standards. She had been in her very early thirties when it suddenly occurred to her that she hadn't actually got everything and that it would be 'cool' to have a family. Never short of men friends – though a little light on the number of women in her social circle - she'd decided this was the next thing to do. Luke had been the victim and Sunny the product.

'Luke Holland never knew what hit him. Happily carousing his way to oblivion among friends of similar persuasions, he had realised turning thirty that this just couldn't go on. He didn't know what to replace it with and, having no long-term girlfriend at that time, was beginning to move away from pure hedonistic pursuits to moments of quiet reflection where he pondered his next life-changing event. As a successful IT consultant who was very much in demand, he was happy professionally. He was also financially independent. Still, if he had been asked to gauge his happiness level he would have said: 'Content, but…' He was ripe for the taking.

'That was when he caught the eye of Janey and in a desperation of tender feelings, that he believed they both shared, they married. It was a convenient marriage too, as they both worked for the same company at that time and, for a while, he thought he'd got it made.

'Then the broodiness Janey felt intruded. At first he had resisted this foray into family building but, as with most things in this marriage, he eventually applied his laid-back style to the 'problem' and went along with what Janey wanted. Within a year Janey had given birth to Sunny and all had appeared set for a state of 'happy-ever-after'.

'Unfortunately, it was at this juncture that a number of events in her past, which had moulded her character to date, conspired to resurface and rebel. The catalysts were various: her promotion to a senior level that was really beyond her ability to cope; having to discuss rather than issue orders to her laid-back husband, and; the difficulties brought about by even her vestigial involvement in the upbringing of her child. From the outgoing, if manipulative, twenty-or-thirty something loved by most, had evolved a dark, sour, damaged human being.

'In short order, Luke took charge. First, he began doing some of his work from home but then, railing against Sunny being looked after by strangers, decided to leave paid employment and look after his child and household full time, taking only what 'contract' work he could do at home. Only recently he had embarked on the diversion of writing, which helped erode the drabness of his existence outside his time with Sunny and filled, in part, the void left by his vacating a creative full-time job.

'All these changes to Luke's life freed Janey from close involvement in the marriage and family life. She could soar in her well-paid job with little restriction from the home front. Unfortunately, she wasn't soaring, she was floundering and that was an entirely different situation for Luke to deal with. There had been three warnings so far and the fourth was now making itself known. He knew their situation could not continue. He had to act.'

The door to Janey's office was open and the sounds from the secretaries in the corridor were clearly audible, if not intrusive to a normal audience. But Janey and her PA were not a normal audience. They were very busy, working on a sheaf of papers and answering phones.

Martin entered the room.

Janey looked up, tension in her face as she recognised him. 'Martin,' she said, holding up her hand. 'I know what you're going to say.'

Janey walked around her desk towards him. Claire left the room without, this time, requiring any signal. She closed the door behind her.

Martin waited for this to complete before turning back to face Janey. His tone was cold, angry. 'Don't ever presume you know what I'm going to say,' he snarled. 'Where's Gerry?'

'He's sitting in on the Change Board for me while I get tonight's launch sorted. He should be finished soon.'

Martin looked at his watch. '*You'll* have to tell him, then,' he decided, aloud. 'Your fix last night seems to have worked. Unfortunately, it doesn't seem to have stopped the markets giving us stick. The board have decided to call in a systems house to hold our hands for a while.'

Janey groaned. 'The knee-jerk response. How will that help, Martin? We've seven more launches over the next two months. By the time they get their feet under the table we'll have finished. Or we would have if they weren't here building another empire.'

'You know that and I know that, but the markets want to see us doing something. Getting the systems house in will calm their nerves.'

'Then we'll never get rid of them.'

'Deal with today. Remember, it was your department that screwed up.'

'It wasn't my department, Martin. Some trader got his pet developer to stick a fix in for him. It clobbered the release.'

Martin didn't reply. He just turned away and walked to the door before turning back again to face her. 'A team of four will be arriving this afternoon. I want you to give them every assistance.'

Janey waved a hand across her desk. 'I don't have time to baby-sit, Martin. I'm in the middle of a release.'

Martin shrugged. 'Find time.' He shut the door forcibly behind him.

Janey put her head in her hands. Then she covered her mouth as she retched. She headed for the door and flung it open.

She rushed down the corridor and through a door marked: 'Women.'

Around the office, people chattered among themselves in a quiet, conspiratorial manner, occasionally looking at the door that Janey had just used.

From behind the door came the sound of more retching before, several minutes later, Janey emerged. She looked pale and walked unsteadily back to her office and slammed the door.

The tantrum she threw on her return to her office was not spectacular but it *was* spectacularly out of character. It was also something of an anti-climax after she had slammed the door shut.

What followed was a feeble, pathetic attempt at destruction brought about by desperation and frustration. Janey tried to trash her office, which was to her – however mistakenly – the reason for her situation. Still it was a subdued, almost controlled, and token destruction.

She first swept all the things on her desk onto the floor and followed this by throwing a coffee cup from the conference table at the wall.

Then she noticed the photograph of Luke and Sunny, now on the floor with its glass broken. She picked it up disinterestedly and put it on her desk.

Finally, she returned to her seat and stared straight ahead. She began to rock back and forth.

Claire hurried along the corridor towards Janey's office, in response to the noise of the slamming door. As she passed Steve's work area, he smiled. Then he looked furtively about himself before returning his gaze to his computer screen.

When Claire entered Janey's office, Janey was sitting behind her desk and staring at the large picture on the wall. There were tears on her cheeks. She had her arms wrapped around her and continued to rock gently back and forth.

Claire walked slowly towards Janey, a little scared.

She didn't get there. Another woman entered. This was Gerry's PA. She was older and moved Claire gently but firmly to one side. 'It's all right. I'll deal with this,' she said, quietly.

Then she looked closely at Janey and nodded slowly, regret in her eyes.

Janey didn't appear to notice any of this, but continued rocking and focusing on the painting on the wall.

Gerry was just entering his office when his PA approached down the corridor. They went into his office and she closed the door. Her expression was serious.

'We've got a problem,' she said, quietly. 'It's Janey. You'd better come.'

Gerry smiled at the mention of Janey's name but adopted a concerned look. 'Who's the goddess nailed this time?'

'This goddess has just joined us mortals,' responded his PA.

'Oh.'

The expressions on the faces of the PAs and secretaries were in mass shocked interest as Gerry and his PA walked the three dozen steps to Janey's closed office door.

Janey was still in her chair and rocking to and fro as she stared at the painting on the wall.

A flicker of recognition came to her eyes as Gerry and his PA entered her office but she made no attempt to move from her seat. 'Breaking Waves,' she announced, nodding towards the painting. 'I could do it better than that. I could.'

'You paint, Janey?' Gerry's tone was quiet, peaceful.

Janey looked down. 'Not so you'd notice. But I could do better than that. I've looked at it every day I've been here. Over five years.'

Gerry moved to the desk and sat by Janey.

'That's a long time. You must know it very well by now.'

'Every brush-stroke. Every nuance,' she explained. 'I could.'

'Then why don't you?'

'No time. There just isn't enough time, Gerry.' She was a little girl now and her voice was correspondingly shrill.

'I think we should make some time,' he replied. 'I'd like to see this picture of yours - if you really want to do it.'

'No time,' repeated Janey. She took a deep breath. 'There just isn't enough time.'

Then she held her head in her hands. 'There's just too much to do.'

Gerry smiled, but when he spoke it was with calm but firm assurance. 'Nothing that can't wait. Nothing we can't share among the others for a while. What are contractors for if not to spell the permanent players,' he argued. 'But that picture…'

Gerry moved over to the wall and looked closely at the picture. 'You know, I see what you mean. I'd like you to tackle this.'

Janey spoke in a monotone. 'I could do it.'

Gerry and his PA swapped concerned looks. Then Gerry moved over to Janey and touched her shoulder.

'You know, we spend far too much time looking at the job around here,' he said. 'I've been watching you for some time and I'm afraid I've asked you to take on too much. You've been ill a few times recently. You're probably run down. You need to take some time away from this and I think you've hit the nail on the head with this painting project. Now, you're to go home.'

Gerry glanced again towards his PA. 'A car is waiting. The next time I see you I want it to be with ..,' he pointed at the painting, '…its replacement in your hands.'

When Janey spoke again it was still in the little girl's voice, capitulating. 'I *could* do with a rest, Gerry.'

'Fine. And no rush to get back. Take your time. As long as you need.' Once again he glanced at his PA. 'Now Irene is going to look after you. You must call me if you have any problems.'

As Gerry passed Steve's desk on his way back down the corridor to his office, Steve looked furtively about himself again. Then he picked up his phone and pressed a button. 'It's done,' he said.

Replacing the phone, he turned back to his computer and began typing, his expression neutral.

Gerry paused in the doorway to his office before turning back to one of the secretaries and said, out of earshot of the others: 'Let me have Janey's personnel file, will you?'

Gerry entered his office and closed the door behind him with a sigh. Then he moved over to his desk, removed a small notebook from the inside pocket of his jacket and picked up the phone.

As he began to speak the door opened and Gerry's PA entered with a folder.

'Paul, we have a problem. Janey Holland,' he began. Then: 'Oh, I see. News certainly does travel fast. I'm seeing too many of these, nowadays. Yes, I think it is serious. She's wobbled before but nothing like this ...'

As he spoke, he was looking through Janey's file. 'Yes. Usual routine, please. We need her replacement today.' Then: 'Okay, Paul. I'll have Steve take over her duties for the moment. But I need someone of Janey's calibre soonest.'

Gerry replaced the phone and turned a page in Janey Holland's folder. His finger traced to her home telephone number to rest under the last four digits: 7474. He picked up the 'phone.

'Mr Holland,' he said, then glanced at the folder again. 'Er, Luke?

Chapter Three

Janey was slumped in a large armchair, looking drawn and a little spaced out. She was wearing a blouse with short sleeves and in the crook of her left arm there was a small circular plaster.

Leaning against his desk in front of her, David was watching her closely. 'Relax,' he advised, quietly. 'It's only been two days. The tablets have that effect.'

Janey tried to get up but David put a hand on her shoulder to prevent her from doing so.

'Just go with the flow,' he instructed, gently. 'Don't fight it. And don't tell me you're not fighting it, because I know you too well.' Then he smiled. 'I've often worried that our family friendship would develop into a professional relationship.'

Slurring her words, Janey said: 'You mean you've had your beady head-shrinker eye on me all these years?' Then she began crying. 'You know there's nothing really wrong with me, David. It's just pretty hectic at the office. Nothing I can't...' She paused, a quizzical expression on her face. 'Couldn't usually handle. I don't really understand it.'

'Four times you've been 'just tired' in two years,' he responded. 'Each time worse than before. That isn't just being tired. And now your company knows.

We can't keep it quiet any more. You have to accept treatment.'

'You know as well as I do that's just the company protecting itself.'

'Janey, you threw a bit of a wobbly at work. It is not normal behaviour. This was a step over the edge.

'Why won't you listen, David? I just feel tired.'

David was insistent: 'The brain has had enough. You are probably close to burn-out and if that happens some of the systems that shut down just don't start up again.'

'David!' she pleaded.

'This isn't something you can just ignore, Janey. Your company knows it - enough to pay the bills, anyhow. Luke knows too, although I'm surprised he won the battle and got you here. I know it and I know that you know it.'

'So everybody knows,' she summarised, smiling weakly. Then she sighed. It was a deep and loud release of air. 'I just need some rest. If I can just take a break for a couple more days, I'll cope.'

David's anger rose at her apparent intransigence. 'There you go again; trying to keep control. Relax, Janey. Why is it that people who are otherwise perfectly sensible, seem to think they can cure years of stress with a couple of days rest?'

Janey managed a weak smile. 'Sounds like you could do with a rest, David.'

David did his best to ignore the interruption. 'Janey, you have to behave. Take this development seriously.'

He looked at a document on his desk. Then: 'I've arranged for you to go into a little place which specialises in treating this kind of problem.'

'I've no intention of gawping at four walls in some glorified health farm. I'm an active person. I relax in my own way. What I need is time to relax.'

'In two days?'

'Alright, a few more than two days. I've already decided how I'm going to do it.'

'Oh, you have, have you?' he asked, mildly surprised.

'I'll take a cottage in the country and paint pictures. Back to basics.'

'And you'll have Luke there to care for you. Is that it?'

Janey's expression was evasive. 'Hmm,' was her response.

David shook his head. 'Back in a minute,' he announced and left the room.

Janey stared into space for a second, then she closed her eyes.

In the outer office Luke got up from his chair as David approached. Janey could hear an indistinct conversation between David and her husband through the panelled door. Her expression remained blank, subdued.

When David returned she blinked awake.

David's manner was now business-like. His relationship of friend had gone and his tone was professional. 'I suppose your symptoms aren't yet extreme.'

Then he turned to face Janey. 'What do Luke and Sunny really think of this plan of yours?'

Janey was cagey. 'Luke is very supportive of the idea. Sunny doesn't quite understand.'

'You mean you brow-beat Luke, as usual.' He paused, as if weighing some great decision. 'Ok. If Luke is supporting you - again - then I'm prepared to agree to the plan. I'll give you something to let you sleep.'

'Thank you, David.'

'I'm going to be away for a few days. When I get back we must talk.' He leant forward and touched the small plaster on Janey's arm. 'I'll get the results of the blood test to you too.'

David helped Janey to her feet and guided her to the door, where he paused. 'If I hadn't known you and Luke for so long, and become so intimate with your screw-ball psyche, I wouldn't be caving into your demands. You're close to the edge, Janey. Complete rest is what you need. Take care.'

Janey was sat in her lounge holding a glass of red wine when Luke entered and closed the door quietly. 'Well, she finally got off.'

Then he noticed the glass of wine. 'David said you should lay off the wine for the time being. It won't help. You don't even drink.'

'One glass will be all right. I didn't take any of the pills.'

Luke sighed. 'Good old Janey. Control freak. Do your own thing.'

He picked up a wad of holiday brochures.

'So, where do we want to go? I've got skiing in Canada, safari in South Africa, or I might be able to swing a change of our timeshare slot?'

'I want to be alone.'

Luke looked pained.

'Not permanently, but I want to get away from everything for a short time. Break the cycle.' She noticed Luke's expression of dismay and reached a hand out to touch his arm. 'Of course, it's not fair on you, as usual, but I need to rediscover my sense of perspective.'

'I might have known. You've probably got it all worked out - with your family coming last on your list of priorities as usual,' he responded, making no attempt to hide his disappointment in her.

Janey rubbed her eyes. 'I don't have the strength to argue, Luke,' she mewled. Then: 'We haven't been close for some time...'

'And being apart will bring us closer? Great logic.'

'I need time to think things out,' she pleaded. 'Over the years the person you married has all but disappeared.'

'You can say that again.'

'Part of me has gone missing. I'd like to come back whole again, with no baggage and without putting you and Sunny through any more pain. When I get back things will be different.'

'If you come back...'

They both paused to consider this for a moment.

'As usual you get your own way,' he said, at last. What's the plan? It'd better be good. I'll probably end up organising it.'

Janey dug into her handbag and pulled out a photograph, which she handed to him. 'I want to repaint this scene. I want to go there and paint this scene.'

Luke looked at the photograph, then he turned it over and read aloud the words on the back: 'Breaking Waves. Glennis Head. Cornwall.'

He turned back to look at Janey. 'I see, break the cycle, break the waves. So this is what David meant.' He shrugged, embarrassed. 'I just back-peddled blindly and said I supported you.'

Janey smiled, weakly.

Luke's expression was cold. 'Okay, I'll organise it. When do you want to go?'

'The sooner I go, the sooner I return.'

Luke shook his head. Then: 'You know you're clinging to this idea like it's a lifeline. What if it snaps?'

'What do you mean?'

'Oh, I don't know,' he responded, shrugging his shoulders. Then: 'Yes I do. You're depending on this thing clearing your head, sorting everything out.'

'Luke, I need your help with this. To make it happen. I won't know unless I do it. But I just know I need this time to myself…'

Janey started sobbing. Luke looked on expressionless. 'Ok. I'll organise it,' he said, quietly, through gritted teeth. 'I'll bloody organise it, alright.'

Luke and Janey left the art materials store and were walking along a cold street with large packages in their hands, mostly carried by Luke.

'I once remember you doing a similar thing in a ski shop,' he said. 'You'd never skied before either. Equipped for giant slalom and *après-ski* in one hour. You don't even know how to use half this stuff.'

'I bought a book, didn't I?'

'Let's hope it takes you beyond the artist's equivalent of the nursery slopes. Do you suppose Oxfam take barely-used art materials, too?'

'Careful, your sneer is showing.'

Luke stopped walking but Janey didn't follow suit and so Luke struggled to catch up with her again. 'Can I just say - for the umpteenth time - that I view this venture as distinctly unwise. At least stay in a hotel.'

'No. We haven't time. No hotel. Back to basics.'

Luke shook his head. 'Fine. Tomorrow's the day, then.'

Chapter Four

Luke and Janey were sitting in the back seat of the helicopter as it flew along the coast. She was asleep in the corner away from Luke. Luke was wearing a worried expression as he studied the inhospitable terrain below. Then he heard something in the headset and nudged Janey awake. 'Pilot says we'll be there in a couple of minutes.'

Janey stretched and moved closer to Luke and the scene from his window. The helicopter was flying parallel to the coast but out over the sea. The view was of a rugged coast dominated by small cliffs and beaches. Above the land the sky was leaden with low, dark cloud which had kept the helicopter at low level for the entire journey.

After a few seconds Janey's expression changed from resignation to mild interest. Then she reached for the photograph. 'This is it all right,' she said. 'Just look at those waves... And there's the cottage.'

'It's a lot smaller than I expected,' said Luke, nervously.

The helicopter landed on top of the cliff only feet from the edge. Then a crewman got out and helped Janey and Luke to disembark. The two of them moved away from the rotors, pulling their coats around them against a chill wind which was considerably reinforced by the downdraft.

The helicopter rotors continued spinning while the crewman shuffled between the helicopter and the cottage transferring baggage and stores. Meanwhile, Luke was trying to get Janey's attention to tell her something but it was all she could do to recognise his presence, so taken was she with the view of the cliffs that she recognised from the 'Breaking Waves' painting.

Luke tried again, shouting even louder this time. 'Are you sure about this? You're hardly the most practical of people.'

Janey appeared restless, irritated. 'Luke. Just go. Go. Go. Go.'

He grabbed her to give her a kiss but she moved her head to one side and instead of on the lips it landed on her cheek. Undaunted, he pressed a small oblong frame into her hand. 'Here's a list of things you need to know about,' he shouted, above the noise. 'Read them. They'll help you know if you are getting better – or not.'

'I don't need anything else,' she cried, exasperated, and threw the frame to the ground.

Though hurt by this action, Luke just shrugged and turned towards the waiting helicopter, his patience at an end.

As the helicopter revved-up and took up the hover, Janey looked from the cliffs to the machine, and gave a perfunctory wave before turning abruptly towards the cottage.

Luke's expression was miserable and he didn't avert his gaze from his departing wife as she strode to the cottage until the turn of the helicopter cabin cut her off from his sight. When he turned his gaze inside the cabin his expression was unambiguous. He was frightened.

With the helicopter gone the noise level was much less, although there was now the sound of the waves on the rocks below the cliffs and the wind which rattled the unsecured door of the cottage.

Inside,, Janey spent a few seconds looking around the place. The gear: duvet, pillows, clothes, food store, had been piled haphazardly into a couple of mounds, together with the painting bits, to which she quickly added her parka.

She noticed a torch on the top of the pile. In the gloom of the cottage she clicked it on and off idly and distractedly. Her inspection was perfunctory, just going through the motions.

The cottage appointments were very basic, just a ground floor and two actual rooms. To a more critical eye the entire building appeared little no more than a brick shed. The inside walls were whitewashed and only one small window cast minimal light into the room.

Janey opened the only internal door onto a very basic bathroom-cum-toilet at the kitchen end of the building. Unimpressed, she closed the door quickly.

A couple of strategically placed hurricane lamps punctuated the overhead in the main room, each dangling from a beam by a length of string, and a gas-ring embellished the one outside wall working surface to the side of a caravan-sized sink with its caravan- sized tap.

From the gas-ring, an orange-coloured rubber pipe snaked out through the wall. Next to this stood a cupboard with a fine-mesh door housing a few bits of crockery, including a small selection of cutlery.

The kitchen was divided from the lounge by the breakfast bar, an eighteen-inch wide plank some four feet long which jutted out into the room opposite and to the right of the only outside door.

A dog-eared and stained document marked 'Inventory' lay on the breakfast bar close to the wall. Attached to it by string was a pencil.

The lounge and its divan settee took up most of the remainder of the internal space of some ten feet by twelve.

In one corner stood a tall but narrow clothes closet, and an armchair, small table, small bookcase (resplendent in faded paperbacks), and a small radiant-heat portable gas-fire completed the furniture.

There was no carpet, just a criss-cross of uneven quarry tiles, caked in old red polish and between which there was no mortar. There was a faded decay about the property and there was a musty smell, suggesting it had been unoccupied for an extended period.

As she completed her initial perusal, reality began to hit home. 'I suppose I *did* want to return to basics,' she said aloud, in justification for her current situation. A chill gripped her then and she donned her parka again.

Then she remembered her mission, which bucked up her spirits somewhat. She rifled through her belongings and emerged with a sketchpad and pens. 'It's still light out there so what are we waiting for?'

As she walked towards the cliff, Janey pulled from her pocket the photograph of the 'Breaking Waves' painting.

Her first task, she decided, was to find the vantage point that would reveal the scene in the photograph. What ensued was in stark contrast with her normal efficiency. To be fair, her efficiency was in business management and this was another world. There she was an expert, in the practical world out here on the cliffs she was a novice.

Like some Charlie Chaplin farce she scooted along the cliff as she sought to locate the view which coincided exactly with the scene depicted in the photograph. First she stopped at the cliff edge, looking theatrically right then left. She turned right and walked along the cliff, halting occasionally to compare the photograph with the view.

She stopped again, looked left then right, holding up the photograph to compare it with the view. Then she walked along the cliffs a few yards and checked the view again.

Having failed to match photograph with any scene so far, she shook her head, exasperated, and threw her hands in the air—but she didn't give up. Determinedly, she turned round and marched back along the cliff.

As before, she occasionally stopped to compare the photograph with the cliffs. At a particular point she brightened. The scene between the photograph and the view matched. 'Yes!' she cried, in exultation.

Scouting around, but always with one eye on the exact spot on the ground where she first matched the photograph and view, she collected and put stones at the spot, building a small cairn.

Still searching for yet another stone she glanced up from the ground for the first time – and noticed the cottage was right in front of her.

She threw the stone on the cairn. 'Bloody fool,' she told herself. 'Even I can find this spot again without a marker!'

A few minutes later she staggered away from the cottage carrying an expensive easel and chair.

She erected the easel and chair by the cairn of stones, and put her sketchpad and pens on the seat. Then she clipped the photograph into the top of the easel.

The wind was gusting by now and, in no time at all, the photograph was plucked away, to sail out over the cliff to lodge in coarse grass some twenty feet below the top of the cliff.

Janey watched it all the way down, groaning inwardly. Undaunted, she moved tentatively to the edge of the cliff and began to attempt an impossible descent.

Holding on to a sprig of vegetation which was, itself, clinging on to the rock with it's fingernails, she was almost at the point of losing her footing on the loose scree when she sensed rather than saw something fall past her. As she looked down she saw the easel, chair, and sketchpad tumble all the way onto the rocks at the bottom of the cliffs. As a final act, the photograph—just inches from her outstretched hand—dislodged from its temporary lodging in the grass and flew out over the sea to disappear from view against the grey and white sea background below.

For a moment-or-so she clung immobile against the sheer wall of cliff, her eyes closed. Then she felt dizzy and her legs began to shake from the strain of maintaining her position. She determined to move immediately and, after a scramble, was quickly back on the top of the cliff. Although she was physically shaking, she did not feel any fear or horror at what might have been the result of her foolish action.

She did feel anger, however. In a comical performance, all the more so as what she said was plucked away by the wind, she threw a tantrum. Fists were raised and she railed against imagined opponents, so great was her frustration.

Then she sat on the ground and hit the bare sod with her fists for a minute-or-so until she had calmed down. After she had wiped the tears from her eyes her head slumped to her chest in resignation.

For several minutes she sat, disconsolate and looking at the ground for the most part but occasionally looking at the waves crashing on the rocks at the bottom of the cliff. Then she raised her head to look at the desolate landscape to the East.

She shivered. 'What a dismal place,' she said, with feeling, and continued to stare ahead. She looked at her watch. 'Everything ruined and I've barely been here an hour!'

Gradually, she became aware of a golden glow on the ground around her. Her interest was piqued and she struggled to turn around to investigate. But she didn't put too much effort into the move, merely turning to lie on her front.

What she saw took her breath away.

The sky to the west was cloudless in a narrow band just above the horizon. For two short minutes she watched the sunset and was taken aback by the beauty of the countryside now bathed in the Sun's soft rays. Because of the angle of the Sun's rays, so late in the day, there were deep shadows at every feature in the rugged landscape, topped by gold. The scene was such a wonderful contrast to the sombre view just minutes before. Again the rollercoaster of her moods swung upwards and she walked towards the cottage in a much improved frame of mind.

As she approached where the helicopter had landed she saw something glint in the grass. She stooped and picked up a small oblong picture frame, the object Luke had tried to give her. There was no photograph, just something printed where a photograph would usually be located. In the half-light it was difficult to read. She could only discern one word, at the bottom: *Luke*.

'Another one of your nonsenses,' she said, suddenly irritated. Without looking at it further she stuffed the frame into the top pocket of her parka and continued towards the cottage.

Janey tried to fill the tiny kettle with water. Nothing came from the tap at first. Then she traced the water pipe to the on-off valve, at which point she could use the pump. The water came from a drum at the side of the house, which was filled from the roof rainwater drainage system. Such details were completely unknown to her; all she knew was that she now had water coming out of the tap. That was as practical as she ever thought it was necessary to be.

Then she placed the kettle on the hob and tried to light the gas. Even though she turned the hob gas-tap there was no spark. She had never used a gas-hob without an ignition source built-in, and that rarely. There was a piezo-electric gas igniter with the cutlery but she would never recognise one unaided. Instead she looked around for a match and found a box by the gas-ring. She wasted two or three matches on the gas-ring before figuring out that no gas was coming out. Eventually she traced the rubber pipe to the wall.

Rummaging around, she picked up the piezo-electric lighter thinking it was a torch and noticed the filaments light when she clicked it on. 'Ah,' she said, and laid it down by the stove. Then she located the torch and went out to find the gas bottles.

Janey searched for and located the gas bottles and switched them both on. While she was outside she looked behind the cottage and saw the one small window in the back wall. She rubbed the glass and noticed that the window frame was open. She made a note to secure it when she got back inside. Then she looked through onto the pile of clothes. The view inside was quite dim even in contrast to the outside visibility of a rapidly approaching sunset.

She turned and worked her way back to the cottage door over the uneven, rock littered ground, noticing the water barrel en route. Off to the side, some feet from the outer wall was a round manhole cover, which was embossed with the word 'sewage'. 'Ah, ' she said, reflectively. 'So that's where that goes.'

Having entered the cottage and shut the door, she shivered. Then she wrinkled her nose. 'It really stinks in here. Never noticed it before.'

Unheard by Janey, against the intrusive noise of the waves on the shore was the hiss of gas coming from the hob. Approaching the hob, she turned the knob on the gas hob which, in fact, now turned it off.

Then she picked up the piezo-electric lighter to light the ring. Before she had pressed the switch she brushed the box of matches off the counter to the floor. As she bent down to pick them up her finger finished pressing the button of the piezo-electric lighter.

There was a flash and an explosion.

For several seconds Janey didn't move and when she did she was dazed and couldn't hear anything. Tentatively, she raised her head above the level of the breakfast bar and got a view of herself in the mirror. Her face was smudged and her hair was wild. Her expression looked oddly shocked but, after some judicious checking of her body, she found she was otherwise unharmed.

Then she looked around the room. The first thing she noticed was that the door was missing. She looked up and noticed a few tiles had been dislodged too. The reason she was able to see the latter was because the tar-paper which divided the room from the underside of the roof was sundered, the shredded edges hanging down in festoons.

She put her hand against her ear, tapping it slightly as she tried to restore hearing.

Then she moved over to the window, where the window frame had been blown back against the outside wall in the blast - shattering the panes - and went to close the venetian-blind type shutters and curtains. Unfortunately, the blinds were now in tatters.

There was no emotion; she was still dazed. Stunned, she just looked around the place and noted the damage casually and superficially. She pulled down what bits of the tar-paper she could reach in a half-hearted manner and, having scrunched them up, threw them behind the settee. Then she spent some minutes 'tidying' the place, but with little effect. Finally, she moved back to the sink and poured a cup of cold water. It was not as enticing as the hot beverage she had so recently planned, she reflected, but at least its preparation was less dangerous.

Chapter Five

Janey was sat cross-legged on the divan long after the night had drawn in outside the cottage. Around her shoulders she had draped her duvet. Behind her the hurricane lamps were fizzing and the door was propped-up precariously against the door jamb. The stores and clothes were exactly where the crewman had left them.

Around her were the remnants of her supper and a plate bearing the residue of baked beans was balanced on the arm of the divan. In one hand she was holding a cup of water and, in the other, was her mobile 'phone, pressed against her ear.

'How are things? Settled in?' asked Luke.

Janey looked around her, then went back to looking down at the floor. 'Getting there. A few small problems. How's Sunny?'

'Missing you. So am I.'

Janey saw a flash of light on the wall and turned to the window but there was nothing there.

'Are you still there, Janey?'

'Yes,' she replied, distractedly.

'Is there something wrong?

Janey moved over to the window and saw the curtain waft from the wind through the broken pane. As she moved back to the divan she saw her reflection in the mirror above the sink and imagined a flash of light as she moved across it.

She relaxed. 'No. The wind's getting up and I think it's started raining. I'll call you tomorrow.'

'Have you taken your tablets? You know you should. They'll help you sleep.'

'Yes, yes. All three colours,' she replied. 'Anymore and I'll rattle.' Then she feigned a yawn. 'I think they're working. Bye.'

'Bye, darling.'

Janey turned off her mobile and placed it on the floor next to the divan. Then she looked at her watch. The time was 11:15.

She turned off one of the hurricane lamps, and listened to the rain on the roof and noticed a gust of wind move the curtains.

Then she put the other hurricane lamp on the floor next to the divan before snuggling under the duvet and switching off the lamp.

For a second or two all was just gentle rain and breeze and the sound of the waves below the cliffs. Then the sound of rain became much louder and the drips grew larger and began to bounce off the furniture and floor, arriving there through the openings left by the missing roof tiles.

The largest opening was where the sloping roof met the wall above the window. Janey didn't notice this. She was already asleep.

Now, as the water dripped down the wall it splashed on the window sill. Through the window and against the slight ambient light outside was framed the shadowy outline of a man's head.

The figure at the window moved away presently, stumbling over the uneven ground. After a few yards the figure paused and tested a torch. In the light it revealed his face. It was not an unkind face but, from the troubled expression, may have been unused to the conditions. Then the torch was directed at the ground and the man moved off through the heavy rain.

In the cottage the noise from the wind and rain grew louder as the rain increased, dragging Janey back to consciousness.

In her confused state she struggled to find the matches for the hurricane lamp but stumbled upon the torch instead and switched it on. She saw the rain was descending in cascades onto her duvet. She checked the time 00:20. A large droplet of water splashed on the watch face and, in response she pointed the torch at the roof. The gaps between the tiles were clearly visible and so was the descending rain.

Drowsily she winced at the sight. Then she struggled to move herself and her duvet from under the most forceful cascade and burrowed into the duvet once more.

Outside the wind got even louder but she didn't react to the noise in any way. She was asleep again.

Light streamed through a door-less entrance. The rain had stopped and the wind had died to nothing. The sound of the waves on the shore below the cliffs and the occasional cry of a seagull were the main noises outside.

The scene inside the cottage was of drab devastation. The duvet appeared sodden and it seemed that most of the clothes and furniture were wet.

Eventually the mound of duvet that was part Janey moved tentatively in response to the new noise – the noise of something like pages being torn out of a book. Slowly, her dishevelled hair emerged from the duvet followed by the rest of her head, eyes shut against the bright light. The noise continued, now accompanied by a scraping sound. Janey moved her head towards the noise and finally opened an eye.

Continuing her squint-eyed investigation of the noise, she decided it was coming from outside. Then she did a double take as the head of a pony came into view around a doorframe— a doorframe which no longer had a door.

The pony looked at Janey's slowly emerging form. 'Whatever next?' asked Janey, quietly.

At the sound of her voice the pony withdrew from view.

The pony did not go very far, only to an area of grass a few feet away where it dropped its head to graze.

Inside the cottage, Janey took a brief look around the room before laying her head back on the sodden divan.

'Was this really a good idea?' she asked herself.

Then she heard the pony chewing grass again and her expression brightened.

She was fully dressed under the duvet and quickly disentangled herself. Then she slipped on her shoes, one of which she quickly removed again to drain it of water.

Jany saw that the pony was only fifteen-or-so feet from the cottage. She stooped to pick up some grass and walked to within five feet of her new neighbour.

At this point she stopped and held out the grass. As she waited for a reaction Janey looked over the pony, noting a freeze-mark on its withers and signs of trimming on the hooves.

'Come on, darling,' she encouraged, in a soothing voice. 'You're no wild pony. What are you doing here then, eh?'

Hesitantly, the pony moved forward until he was munching the grass in Janey's hand, all the time remaining on tenterhooks, ready to flee.

Gradually, Janey lowered herself to her haunches, at which point the pony brought his nose to hers and started sniffing. Janey returned the greeting by blowing into one nostril softly.

'Now we've been introduced, perhaps we'll meet again. I used to have a pony just like you. Yes, I did. I'll bet you've won a few prizes. Which lucky little girl or boy do you belong to?'

Janey quietly stood up and, as if at a signal, the pony moved away, trotting and finally cantering away, nickering.

'Good paces, too,' she reflected.

Janey re-entered the cottage and surveyed the inside. With a groan she uttered: 'Whose silly idea was this?' Then: 'Note to self: must stop complaining.'

Then she began clearing up the mess of wet clothing and duvet. As she raised one corner of the duvet she saw a pool of water in the uneven floor. In the middle lay her mobile phone.

'Bloody, bloody, bloody!' she cried, in frustration.

Quickly, but several hours too late, she picked up the phone, grabbed a cloth and began mopping off the water. She was about to press the *On* button when she hesitated. 'Not a good idea,' she said, instead continuing to mop the phone. 'Water and electricity do not mix. Even I know that. We're just going to have to dry you out and hope you work.'

Janey removed the battery from the phone with some difficulty, the two parts of the phone and battery spinning off in different directions but each landing on something soft. Then she wiped the bits and put them on the breakfast table to dry out even more. As she did so, she remembered which bit went where and which side up. She noted that the battery fitted with the number , *8888*, on the reverse side.'

Chapter Six

By mid-morning the cottage looked a little neater, but not much. She had managed to move the mountains of clothes and kit around a bit so that the mountain of clothes was now mainly a mountain of kit and the mountain of kit was transformed into festoons of clothes hung from every place which might intercept a wafting, drying breeze. The unwashed dishes of the previous evening were now a neatly stacked set of unwashed dishes that she intended getting around to soon.

Vaguely pleased with herself at her efforts, she celebrated by holding a cup in her hand and contemplating some food on the breakfast bar at which she sat. When she put down her cup she noticed the document marked 'Inventory'. As she thumbed through it, idly, it revealed a list of instructions for using the gas and other things.

'*Now* you tell me,' she said, disgusted, throwing it down onto the table again.

Then she looked around at the damage from the explosion and rain. It had been difficult to shed the sense of gloom she'd felt the previous evening on seeing the inside of the cottage. Now she wondered how she would cope with the worsening of the aspect she had wreaked upon it—but not for long. 'Ah, sod it,' she said, with feeling. 'Let's go painting.'

She got up from the table and moved over to where the art materials were gathered, what remained of them.

'I really must do a sketch first.' she said. 'A paper and pen would be handy.'

She looked around hopefully and her eyes found the inventory document again. She picked it up and rifled through it, looking for blank sheets. There were none, but she did notice that only one side of each page was printed on. The other was completely blank.

'Why not?' she asked herself and looked at the pen, which was attached by string. 'Even better. It comes with a pencil, too.'

Minutes later, after dressing, Janey was staggering awkwardly away from the cottage, carrying the armchair to the spot she had marked with stones. She'd got it upside-down and balanced on her head where the seat cushion should have been. Unfortunately, the back of the chair had twisted round so that it was in her face and she struggled to get it turned round so that she could see where she was going before moving a little less unsteadily forward.

At the cairn she dropped the chair heavily into place and retrieved the inventory/sketch pad from down her trousers. She was wearing a scarf and parka, gloves and boots, and got herself extravagantly comfortable with the makeshift sketchpad opened in front of her and the pen poised. Then she waited for the vibrant flush of inspiration that must surely overwhelm her imminently.

It seemed to her that she'd been sat there for an age before the blank page bore any change. But eventually a doodle formed in the top right hand corner, little more than a scribble and nothing like the sketch she was trying to achieve in this session. This state of affairs lasted no more than a minute but instead of developing into something more grand was stillborn when she angrily despatched the paper to the limited breeze.

She shook herself and this initiated a spurt of activity which saw her insert a clever doodle in the top left hand corner of the page. It was joined some minutes later with a large St. Andrews cross, across the whole page, applied with angry gusto, but this too soon joined the other as a plaything of the wind.

She closed her eyes then. All the problems she had faced came back to haunt her and it seemed were now conspiring to reveal her stupidity. Surely she was continuing her arrogance too far to think she could paint. It was worse than that, she told herself, she couldn't even draw. The tears came and she felt wretched.

After she had sobbed for some time she began to convince herself that the important thing was to just get something, anything, on the page and then just play with it until it became something, er, better. She told herself over and over that time just wasn't of the essence; there was no rush and it did not matter if whatever she created wasn't any good. She reminded herself it wasn't a competition. She would just play with it until it got better – no matter how many times she needed to revise the drawing.

So it was that she began to draw the most unlikely representation of the view before her. Her strokes were deft but did not seem to represent the scene.

Then, as she went over the pencil marks again and again, the sketch became darker and darker and it became difficult to see any picture at all – but what was just discernable was a reasonable representation of the scene before her.

Along the cliff-top, at Janey's back, a man approached. He paused at a distance, unnoticed by Janey as he watched her sketching. Then he looked at the cottage and winced.

Janey sensed his presence and turned around, startled.

The man's reaction registered surprise also. 'Oh, I'm sorry,' he said. 'You appear to have a few slates missing?'

'Pardon?'

The man laughed and approached her. 'Just noticed your cottage roof has a few slates out of place. And your door seems to have come off its hinges.'

Janey appraised the man while he spoke. She tried, futilely, to move a trace of hair into place against the wind. 'A slight accident,' she explained.

'You'd better get it fixed soon,' he counselled. 'It might rain.'

Janey was unimpressed by this. 'It already did,' she said, quietly.

'What?'

Janey smiled. 'I certainly do need to get it fixed. Do you know where there's a phone? I have a mobile but the battery's low.'

The man returned her smile. 'I see. I normally carry one but forgot it today. Actually, I'm always forgetting it. There's a house over there.' He pointed to a rise in the ground, just like many others, but which had the suggestion of a chimney poking out in the dip nearest the coast in the direction from where he'd come. 'D'you see it? They have a phone. You're well off the beaten track here.'

To underline what he said he looked around at the desolate landscape. 'Listen, I should introduce myself, we're neighbours. I've rented the Grange over there ..,' he added, pointing directly inland, '..beyond the hill. Ross White is the name.'

'Janey Holland.'

'I pass this way three or four times a week. It's a nice walk. Clears the brain'.

Ross looked at Janey's sketch. 'Experimental school is it?'

'Just a few ideas,' she responded, haughtily. She rose, hiding the sketch from his view. 'I'd better get someone to repair the cottage before it gets dark.'

Ross laughed. 'You'll be lucky. A month would be optimistic around these parts.'

Janey's face fell.

'If you want, you can stay at my place. Neighbours are a bit thin around here so we tend to stick together'

Seeing Janey's defensive look at this he added, quickly. 'Think about it.'

It was still an awkward moment but he appeared not to know what to say. 'Anyway, better be going.'

Ross turned away, casting a look at the cottage then back to Janey.

'Look, the invitation is real. When it rains you'll be most uncomfortable in there. I have a couple look after me at the Grange. So if I'm not there there'll be someone to let you in.'

Ross walked away shaking his head.

Pausing in her artistic labours only to return to the cottage and boil the kettle for tea - a new skill - Janey was soon back in the armchair, vacuum flask wedged beside her, and holding a sandwich in her non-sketching hand. The sketch, on a new page, was mildly impressive. She had heavily traced the better lines from the original so that they made an imprint on the blank page below. Then she had used that as the starting point for improvements to her sketch. After about an hour more of this she was getting cold and a little tired.

'Enough for now,' she said to herself. 'Any more would spoil it.' She looked at the sky, it was darkening. 'Besides, it might rain. Time to find a repairman.'

She picked up the armchair and put it on her head in the same manner she had used when bringing it from the cottage. Then she walked back towards the cottage via the cliff edge in a rather wobbly fashion. It seemed the cliff edge had a magnetic attraction for her and she came dangerously close to toppling over. Finally, she managing to veer off to the cottage but bumped into the door frame and dropped the armchair in a mess. A leg broke off.

Janey took a little trouble with her appearance before taking the short walk to the cottage Ross had pointed out. Unfortunately, she required a lot of trouble to be taken to repair the damage wreaked by the explosion if there was any chance of her bearing closer scrutiny than had been afforded to Ross White. Although she had lavished cold water and soap on her face it didn't touch her hair and a tidemark was visible at the hairline. Her hair, never totally manageable, was – for want of a better word – 'frizzy' and had at this moment a mind of its own. 'Still, let's not overdo things,' she told herself. 'As far as I know, the Queen hasn't been invited.'

Janey was soon sat in the lounge of her neighbour's cottage. Predictably, it was far smarter than the one she had trashed so comprehensively.

With her was a middle-aged woman called Margaret, who poured the tea and then offered biscuits. Her husband, George, sat by her side, appearing only dutifully interested in this meeting.

'So, you're the new tenant of the cottage,' said Margaret, in a tone that didn't require an answer.

Janey felt she needed to say something, all the same. 'I've taken it for a few weeks to paint some landscapes.'

'We saw the helicopter arrive,' said Margaret. 'Very exciting.'

'One of my husband's contacts owns the company.'

'Oh. We see a few helicopters up and down the coast from time to time. Yellow ones…'

'Air Sea Rescue,' put in George.

'Still,' continued Margaret, 'it's exciting that it should land at the cottage.'

A glance passed between George and Margaret, and he placed a hand on hers. Margaret smiled at Janey but the smile didn't reach her eyes, which were sorrowful. 'And then, last night, we heard a firework go off.'

Janey managed to blush. 'I had an accident… with the gas. Blew the door off and dislodged a few slates on the roof.'

'Heavens. Are you alright?' responded Margaret, genuinely surprised. 'But it really rained last night. How did you keep dry?'

'Not very well. I've come to ask if I can use your phone to call a builder.'

'Oh, yes. You must,' said Margaret, turning to her husband. 'You will do that for Janey, won't you?

George rose slowly, without saying anything, and picked up the phone book before leaving the room.

'You're very kind,' smiled Janey.

'Not at all. What do you plan to paint?'

'The cliffs. I had a picture in my office of this spot, painted some years ago. I thought I would try to better it.' She smiled, apologetically. 'It's in the way of a convalescence after a bad time at work.' Janey looked around the small room, keen to find something, anything to get away from this subject. 'Do you have children?'

'No, not now,' replied Margaret. Then she sighed. 'Once we had a little girl but she died last year.'

'Oh, I'm sorry. I just felt the presence of a child in this room.'

'We've many knick-knacks to remind us of Rosie that we mean to pack away but never seem to. We're sort of getting over it, as much as you can.'

George entered the room. He was carrying a toolbox. 'They'll try and get someone out in the next few days. Waste of time, if you ask me. I'll have a crack at it for you, if you like, but I'm not promising anything?

George and Janey were stood a few feet from the cottage in front of the door and were looking at the cottage. George was wearing a deerstalker hat.

'It should hold until the builder comes,' he announced. Then: 'I could still take a look at those slates over there.'

'No, I won't hear of it,' said Janey, firmly. 'It's much too dangerous and the light's going. The ones you've done were the ones that mattered. It should keep out most of the rain. Thanks again, I very much appreciate what you've done, Mr Smith.'

'You know, you're very lucky to be alive,' he said, carefully. 'Fortunately the door frame was rotten where the hinges are and that made it easier for door to fall away and release the pressure. Are you sure you're okay? You should see a doctor. I could run you into Milton…'

'I'm okay,' she responded, quickly. 'I had ringing in my ears last night but that seems to have gone. Will the hinges hold? On the door, I mean.'

He shrugged. He might have said: 'Suit yourself,' but instead he said: 'I put larger screws in. It'll hold alright.'

'I'm very grateful for your help, Mr Smith.'

George handed the door-key to Janey and smiled shyly. 'George. It gave the lock quite a wallop when the door blew out. I've bent it back as best I can and it should hold.'

'George it is then,' she agreed. Then she moved away towards the cottage door. 'Bye for now.'

George didn't move at first, just stared after her and then at the roof. Then he looked at the sky, which had grown angry, and heard the first spots of rain tapping as they hit his oiled cotton coat. He moved off, back along the coast.

In the lamp-light Janey was trying to improve the sketch and mark out the painting. She was sat in the armchair, its broken front leg now replaced by an up-turned pan with a book on top. The remnants of meal things cluttered the place. Outside, the rain was beating down and the wind was audible through the broken window.

Unseen by Janey, a dim shape appeared at the window, wearing a deerstalker. Then the figure moved away but made a noise as it disturbed the gas-cylinders.

Janey looked up at the window and, although she saw nothing, got up and closed the curtains. Then she moved over to the door and locked it. She turned and leaned against it. Her expression was troubled but it didn't last long before it turned to concern as her attention was interrupted by a loud, hollow, dripping sound.

Janey looked over to a saucepan placed on the floor in a corner of the cottage. Her expression cleared and she retrieved the pan and took it over to the sink. The dripping was less noisy now but the water continued to run away through the cracks between the floor tiles.

Janey looked at her work and the draining rainwater. 'Far more efficient,' she decided.

After another look around her she draped the duvet over her. 'This is the life,' she said.

Janey looked again at the window for a second or two, wearing a serious expression. 'But not necessarily the place.'

Chapter Seven

It was the following afternoon before Janey returned to her usual spot at the top of the cliff. She had been working on the sketch until about two in the morning and when she woke it was already eleven. She had followed breakfast with a walk along the coast to clear away the cobwebs, she told herself, but really she had wanted to meet the pony again. In any case, she was unlucky; he was nowhere to be seen.

She now had a makeshift easel to add to her collection of stuff out on the cliff top. It was made from a piece of the breakfast bar and the canvas was secured with a couple of big plastic note clips she'd found about the place. Her task today was mapping out the major colour areas for colour match. The sketch transferred from the paper during the night had had to be magnified to fit the canvas and she had made an adequate stab at this task.

After two hours work the painting had progressed somewhat with a range of colours on the palette applied roughly, very roughly, to the canvas. Satisfied, Janey stretched and looked around but ahead to the cliffs and inland. She exhaled contentedly.

'Beautiful,' she exclaimed. 'Why did I never see it before?'

Then she sensed there was something behind her. She turned awkwardly around in her seat to see the pony.

All thought of painting forgotten, Janey scattered bits of paraphernalia to the ground around her as she got to her feet. Moving towards the pony she picked up some grass. The pony, in his turn, moved forward to take the grass.

For some minutes she stroked him and talked to him soothingly. What she said meant nothing but the way she said it meant everything. This was a friend, the pony seemed to know. He was relaxed and comfortable. Eventually, he just turned away and put his head down to the short grass again.

Janey then went back to her painting and the pony grazed in the vicinity, occasionally looking up to see what Janey was doing. Janey in turn looked to see what the pony was doing. She was doing very little work now and, at length, gave a big sigh. 'It's no use. Can't concentrate,' she said.

She rose to her feet abruptly.

The pony moved away abruptly and headed inland at a trot.

Janey looked in the direction the pony was going and imagined she saw some smoke. Then she remembered the invitation.

'Why not? It must be tea-time soon.'

Janey made a further, more determined, attempt to tidy herself and by the time she'd checked in the mirror she was reasonably happy with her appearance. This marked a small but significant improvement in her frame of mind from the lethargy and lack of care for herself that she had previously demonstrated.

Leaving the cottage, she paused to shut and lock the door. Then she turned and walked away, the suggestion of a confident step in her gait and a feeling of being truly alive.

The ground that Janey travelled over to get to the Grange was rough and occasionally she stumbled. On one occasion, she fell into a boggy pool. Then there were several hedgerows through or around which the route was not obvious. It did not help that Janey could not always see her objective because of the various obstacles and had only been given a general direction to go — directly inland from the cliffs. Not feeling confident at her orientating skills she was not prepared to 'box' around obstacles and this meant she crawled through more than one hedgerow without the benefit of a gate as she sought the direct route to her destination.

Such was the retardant effect of various gorses and hawthorn on her hair and clothes, and the change of colour and aroma of her clothes hands and face caused by the contents of the boggy pool, she was in something of a dishevelled state when she finally won the way to the drive gates of the Grange.

It was while she was walking along the drive to the Grange, trying to repair the damage to her appearance caused by her journey, that she noticed a man in the grounds some distance away and to one side of the drive, raking and burning clippings. He stared at her blatantly all the way from coming into view until she arrived at the front door. Janey smiled but felt distinctly uncomfortable.

The front door was opened by a middle-aged woman, who introduced herself as Mrs Armitage, the housekeeper.

'Welcome, Janey,' said Mrs Armitage. 'Mr White told me to expect you. The lecherous old man you saw as you came up the drive is my husband.'

Janey laughed nervously.

Janey and Mrs Armitage glanced over to the man but his reaction to this was to suddenly take a close interest in the fire.

Mrs Armitage's expression was not sympathetic to him as her glance lingered in his direction. But she changed it to a smile when she said: 'Come in, come in.'

Janey was diplomatic: 'I can't fault anyone for looking at me the way I look at the moment. I'm afraid I fell in some mud and got lost in a hedge.'

This was no understatement. A brown stain bisected her body in a diagonal line from her right knee to her left shoulder. Her hands were still stained with the same colour though there was evidence that she had managed to remove most of the goo from them. Her hair was once again a beehive festooned with twigs and leaves and smudges adorned her face and clothes.

Mrs Armitage's expression was kind. 'We'll have to do something about that.'

'Is Mr White in?'

Ross entered the hall. 'He certainly is. Welcome.'

'I'll make some tea,' said Mrs Armitage.

'Excellent idea,' said Ross and motioned to the door. 'Come through,' he said, appearing to be only mildly taken aback by her appearance.

Mrs Armitage left.

'Who won?' he enquired.

'Won?'

'The war. You look as if you've been in a fight.'

'A slight altercation with the flora around here, that's all.' She repeated what she had said to Mrs Armitage.

'Why don't you, er, freshen up in the downstairs bathroom,' he suggested. 'I'll ask Mrs Armitage to get you something to wear while we do something with your clothes.'

Half-an-hour elapsed before she returned. She was wearing a skirt that wasn't particularly flattering but was at least dry. 'That was absolutely wonderful,' she announced. 'My first bath in days.'

Ross indicated the settee. 'Please. Take a pew. I passed your way about nine this morning but you weren't about.'

'Didn't sleep too well. Then overslept.'

'Not surprised with the cottage in its current state. Although I noticed that the door was back on and the slates aren't in quite such disarray as yesterday. So at least you got a builder out. You must tell me how you did that. It must be some technique!'

'George Smith…'

Ross looked up at the name, his expression suddenly guarded.

'..from the cottage along the coast,' she continued to say. 'He patched it up while he's trying to get a builder for me. Not perfect but fairly dry in the right places - and I can now lock the door which is a great help. Margaret, his wife is very nice.'

'Yes, I know quite a bit about them. Did she mention their daughter?'

'Very sad,' she volunteered, noting that a tension had entered his voice.

Janey looked around the room, her standard defensive device. 'This place is splendid. You said you rent it?'

Ross nodded, the tension in his voice easing. 'And it comes with Mrs. Armitage and her husband, who relieve me of any of the chores. I just get on with my work.'

'What do you do?'

'I write,' he responded. Then he paused before adding: 'Er, fiction. Crime fiction. Sometimes I write faction - or true stories with a bit of padding.'

'Fascinating. So does my…' She forgot what she was going to say. It had been happening more and more. Still, with repetition had come quicker recovery so that it wasn't so obvious. She imagined it was something to do with stress, but couldn't be sure. She found herself saying: 'Is that what you're doing at the moment, faction?'

Ross nodded again. 'A murder. Local story about a girl who died by falling off her horse and over the cliffs.'

'This girl was murdered? What? Pushed?'

'Something like that. I'm still researching the facts.'

'And this is a true story? I don't think I've heard anything of this.'

'Yes. And yes,' he responded unclearly, 'you have heard something about it. If only obliquely. The girl is the daughter of Mr and Mrs George Smith.

'Oh.'

'Oh, it is,' confirmed Ross. 'Or should be. Alas, I'm the only person who thinks it *is* murder. But as soon as I saw the newspaper report of the inquest I knew there was something wrong. I just have to prove it.'

'But the police? Haven't they got reservations about how she died too?'

'Don't appear to. They went through the motions but it was a sloppy job all round. Plenty of scope for a reinterpretation of evidence.'

'By yourself?'

He nodded. 'Fortunately for me, the public like a convincing story, so I provide one. In this case the evidence presented at the inquest left the coroner with no alternative to a verdict of death by misadventure. I think it should have been declared an open verdict. That would have demanded further investigation. Instead, it was convenient, economic, and pre-sented a verdict that did nothing for justice and everything for social indifference. I mean to get to the bottom of this.'

'Of the cliff?' Janey was horrified at this and couldn't believe she had said it. 'Oh, I'm terribly sorry.'

Ross looked astounded for a moment but then he smiled. 'You're right to poke fun. I can be quite pompous when I get started. But I tell you....'

What Ross had been about to say was stillborn when they heard a commotion in the hallway. Then the front door shut.

In response to this interruption Ross got up and looked through the window. Mr Armitage was walking away carrying a brace of rabbits.

At that moment Mrs Armitage entered, carrying a tray with the tea things on it.

'Sorry about that,' she said, putting down the tray. 'My husband tried to bring his trappings through the front door.' She smiled at Janey. 'You'd think after ten years of marriage he'd be trained by now.'

As she stood up from fiddling with the tea things, Mrs Armitage addressed Janey. 'Will you be staying for dinner?

'Yes,' said Ross, quickly. Then he turned to Janey. 'You must.'

'Thank you, but no. I need to get back to do some detail work on the paintings this evening. Besides, I'm beginning to fall under the spell of this house and need to tear myself away before it is too late.

'The offer is still there. You could do your painting here. There's bags of room. Of course, you'll put on lots of weight from Mrs Armitage's cooking.'

'I also need to be going before it gets dark. It is bad enough walking around here when it's light.'

'Okay,' surrendered Ross, who turned to Mrs Armitage. 'There's your answer, unfortunately.'

Mrs Armitage left then and Ross turned back to Janey. 'Let's have some tea and then you'll just have time for a quick tour before you go. We may yet convince you to stay.'

Janey and Ross chatted as they walked through the deserted stables. It was clear from his behaviour that Ross was as much a stranger there as Janey was.

He tried a door but it was locked.

They both searched the area but it was Janey who found a key and opened the door.

'It's a tack room,' pronounced Janey.

Ross and Janey entered the room. It was sparsely populated with kit but had a full set of tack and grooming kit.

Janey sniffed the tack. 'This has recently been cleaned.'

She then picked up some saddle soap. 'It's still wet,' she said, surprise in her voice.

Ross shrugged. 'I can't think why. As you've seen, we have no horses here.'

Janey looked closely at the bridle. 'Quite a small horse, too,' she added. Then she shivered. 'Cold in here, isn't it?'

Minutes later Janey and Ross strolled slowly down the drive.

'Don't you feel lonely, or scared being on your own in that shabby cottage?' Ross was serious.

'I haven't felt lonely so far. As for being scared, I'm fine except when I let my imagination get the better of me.'

'Sounds like you've had a fright already,' soothed Ross.

Janey smiled weakly. 'Not much more than any *towney* feels when they come to the big wide country-side. We can take the clamour of traffic and people, but we have a problem with the hoot of an owl.' She paused, her expression reflective. 'Although I keep imagining someone is looking through the window.'

Ross managed to conceal his expression from Janey, which was one of surprise. 'I'm no country person myself,' he said, quickly. 'You wouldn't get me living out there.'

'Really?'

'Not when I can have all the luxuries that this place provides.'

'You'd better stop that, I'm beginning to weaken.'

Ross smiled. 'Good! But for now, don't forget the way back, the way I told you.'

They had reached the gate at the end of the drive now and with a wave, Janey moved on while Ross stayed to look after her, disappointed at their parting.

Janey turned back once and waved again before turning back towards the cottage. Her expression brightened. 'Not bad,' she said. 'Not bad at all.'

Chapter Eight

Janey was preparing a meal. It was a tortuous exercise. Pausing briefly, her expression was one of distraction. 'I gave up silver service for this? I must be sicker than I thought.'

While something was boiling to destruction in a pan, Janey began to review her progress with the painting. She looked for something among the papers. 'No, Janey,' she decided. 'The sketch isn't here.'

She straightened from her crouched position. 'Oh, hell. It's got to be around here somewhere!'

The saucepan boiled over and Janey, without any sense of urgency, removed it from the hob and plonked the contents onto the plate. The meal didn't look particularly appetising, but she didn't seem to notice.

She switched off the gas and collected everything onto a board she used for a tray. It was something of a hotchpotch but her expression didn't register any concern at this.

Then she sat down and ate mechanically and without interest for a few mouthfuls before pushing the plate away. She opened the well-thumbed 'How to paint' book and settled down to read.

At the window a face appeared. The features were in shadow but the outline of a deerstalker hat was unmistakable. Janey didn't see it but was uncomfortable and turned around to look at the window. By this time the face had gone. She turned back, wrapping the duvet more tightly about her and continued her reading.

Luke replaced the phone.

He nodded several times, slowly and reflectively. 'So far, so good.'

Then he moved over to, and sat down heavily in, an armchair.

Behind him a figure placed a hand on his shoulder.

The hand belonged to Steve and Steve's expression was tense. 'So far,' he confirmed.

Janey opened the door and shielded her eyes against the daylight. She was untidy, having only just got out of bed, and was carrying a cup in one hand and some pills in another.

As she was about to put the tablets in her mouth she looked around and her face brightened. The pony was standing a few yards away.

'Hello,' she said, quietly.

The pony looked up and moved nearer.

Janey put all the pills in her mouth and sipped the water before swallowing. Then she pulled a face.

She looked again towards the pony. 'I have a feeling you're doing me more good than this lot.'

Janey stooped to get some grass and offered it to the pony. The pony took it.

She scratched the pony's withers and stroked its back. Then Janey's expression became reflective. 'I wonder,' she said, aloud. Then she nodded her head. 'Yes. I think so. I may be a bit heavier but I used to be able to do it. You wait there.'

With this she disappeared into the cottage.

When Janey emerged she was dressed in her 'best alternative to proper riding dress.' In her hand was the internal washing line now fashioned into the shape of a head-collar and reins.

The pony accepted the head-collar without fuss and was quietly led by Janey to a small mound cut out of the peat. This was the most significant feature in the area. She used it as a mounting block.

As Janey sat atop the pony she suffered a lack of balance and to an accompanying shriek from Janey – and quick sidestep from the pony - she fell off the same side she had got on and onto the soft ground.

Possibly because she was still holding onto the reins, the pony didn't stray. Instead he looked down at her, then nuzzled her face, before moving his head to one side and chewing at the grass.

Janey lay there for a moment on her back.

'Bare back riding never was just like riding a bike,' she muttered. 'The important thing to do is to get right back on.'

Janey got back on and after a few steps fell off again. She looked quizzical. 'Better. Definitely improving.'

Then Janey groaned and rubbed her hip as she got to her feet again.

Janey was determined not to give up. When next she mounted, moments later, she stayed on for a few short steps before she was unceremoniously dumped again. This happened a few more times, the pony patiently eating grass each time Janey interrupted her riding with a crash landing to earth with something other than her feet.

As she gazed at close quarters into the eye of the pony, still quietly munching grass by her head as she lay on the ground, she said: 'I know. You're thinking: what an idiot!'

Untroubled by this presumed slight, the idiot got to her feet again and remounted.

Gradually her wild commands became quieter and soon she was doing a trot, bouncing around at first but gradually the dim memories translated into self-preservation in this gait and she remembered and executed the rising trot. She didn't stay in this gait for long, however, as the muscles unused for so many years rebelled at the effort required to do rising trot without the use of stirrups.

She reflected, rather later than was prudent, that she needed to know how to stop, given that there was no bit in the bridle she had constructed to assist with this rather important manoeuvre. Fortunately, the pony was more reluctant to go than to stop and it only took a lessening of the pressure on his sides to halt forward movement at the walk. In fact, it was hard work keeping him going in this gait.

She found she was breathing heavily from the exertion and paused, bringing the pony to a halt. She was pleased with herself. 'Well, that's the walk and trot sorted out.'

She brushed some grass and a smudge from her face. 'Let's see what we remember about the canter.'

At first the pony went into trot and just accelerated in this gait. Eventually he fell into canter and, as Janey slid wildly from side to side on the pony's bare back, the direction changed from safely inland to a direct line to the cliff edge.

It was at this juncture that the rules changed. In walk and trot a reduction in side pressure with her legs caused the pony to decelerate to a stop almost instantaneously. This didn't appear to be the case in canter.

Despite Janey's best efforts to turn or slow the pony, not having use of a bit, the pony went towards the cliffs.

Alarmed, Janey baled-out to one side.

Almost instantly, the pony stopped in its own length, still some distance from the cliff edge.

The breath had been knocked out of Janey and it took a second or two for her to recover. 'Good to see my 'Oh, Christ' stop still works,' she gasped.

Janey looked at the pony, who was calmly chomping on the sparse grass on the edge of the cliff.

'You're a very good pony,' she croaked. 'Shame about the gears and steering.'

Janey mounted again and, pointing him firmly inland, got into a walk and then trot and then – by some miracle of memory – applied the correct aids for the canter and the pony went straight into a controlled hand canter. After a few strides she brought him back to the walk just by thinking trot, sitting quietly, and holding the bridle - *sans* bit – in a 'resisting' hand, and they were soon walking the short distance to the cottage, where Janey dismounted.

'Nice to know you have brakes,' she said, patting him on the neck.

She removed the head-collar and the pony wandered off. As he did so, Janey limped to the cottage door. Then she looked back at the pony one more time and smiled before entering the cottage.

After lunch—something really interesting from a tin—Janey spent some time making changes to the picture. It was as she was doing this that she heard nickering sounds outside.

She didn't look round, concentrating as she was on the picture. 'Can't come out to play, yet. I'm busy,' she called out. But the draw was too much and, within minutes, she put down her work.

Janey emerged from the cottage, blinking in the brighter light. She was looking for the pony. At first she couldn't see him but then saw his shape farther away.

He was lying down with his back to the cliff, looking inland. Janey tried to approach him, keeping low, in the hope that he would stay down until she arrived. He was having none of it: he rose in an ungainly stagger and was shaking himself off by the time Janey arrived by his side.

'No, you're right,' she admitted, soothingly. 'We're not yet good enough friends. After all, we've really only just met.'

Back in the cottage, Janey was rummaging around the pile of sketches but seemed unable to locate something. Then her hand alighted on a piece of paper, her first sketch.

Janey held up the paper. 'Oh, it's you.' Then she looked at it for a moment. 'Well, you're no good. You're the one I lost yesterday. You're too late. I'm looking for another piece of paper today.'

She rummaged through the papers once more, but her search was unsuccessful.

'Oh, well, I'll work on something else,' she said, addressing the cottage generally, 'until you turn up!'

While she was working on her sketch she suddenly paused and smiled, then returned to the sketch.

Instead of working on the sketch though she started doodling until she had formed the outline of a pony. It was not a work of art, more a stick pony.

She looked at it for a moment then drew a heart by it. After a second-or-so of perusal, she drew a stick figure of a man. Again, she considered her work.

Janey sighed and turned back to her work on the sketch. 'One new thing at a time.' Her face bore a far-away look. 'But which?'

Janey was about to turn in and had all the bedclothes organised when a hurricane lamp spluttered and died.

She was alarmed at the sudden decrease in the light, not sure what had happened.

After a moment of hesitation she looked closely at the hurricane lamp, shook it, and realised that it was out of fuel.

Janey relaxed. 'Final confirmation. You are a nervous wreck.'

In the way that people who have done something silly look around to see if anyone noticed, Janey's glance automatically went to the window. A face appeared there but the detail could not be made out.

Janey screamed, paralysed with fear. For a moment-or-so she was rooted to the spot. Then she managed to move over to the door and lock it, before moving to the curtains and pulling them closed

Her glance rested on the bits of the mobile phone on the breakfast table. She grabbed the two halves and was about to join them together when a drop of water leaked from it, splashing onto the floor.

Janey groaned with disappointment, knowing that if she proceeded now with trying to use it she'd probably blow the circuits. She put the two halves and the battery back on the table.

Dissatisfied with the state of her defences she looked around for something to barricade the door. The tall slim closet was all she could use and she wrestled to get it from its place in the corner to the door.

Finally she managed to tilt it against the door, in the course of which manoeuvre the top deposited a large amount of dust and a biscuit tin.

Amid the cloud of dust the biscuit tin crashed to the floor and the lid flew off. A number of pieces of paper and photographs flurried to the floor.

Janey ignored them, her own protection being her only priority. With a final heave the closet jammed at forty-five degrees against the door.

With this, Janey subsided to the divan, tired yet wildly alive. She tried to reassure herself that the danger was past, but was still breathing in short sharp breaths that told her otherwise.

'Keep calm,' she told herself. 'He's probably gone. That was no illusion. He was definitely there. Perhaps he was there before. He could have been watching me since I got here!' She pulled the duvet cover around her shoulders even tighter. 'Well, there's no way I'm going anywhere until morning.'

She struggled to her feet and retrieved a knife from the breakfast bar – it was one of those wide rounded blade dinner knives with the plastic handle. It was of little use as a weapon. Nevertheless she took it back to the divan and sat down. There she held the knife vertically from her hand, which was buried in the duvet.

On her face was a determined, wide-awake, expression.

The morning light filtered through the closed curtains and the sound of a pony nickering caused the mound that was the duvet to move slightly.

Janey's face emerged but her eyes were still closed and her expression was relaxed.

She wriggled comfortably and then murmured: 'Yes, Ross.'

Janey was sprawled on the divan, the duvet lay over her and untidily to either side of her. The knife was on the floor.

Her eyes flickered awake slowly, until she was suddenly wide awake and alarmed. She sat up quickly, listening intently. Then she saw the knife and the events of the night before came back to her with a shock.

Janey went to the door and listened without opening it. Then she donned her shoes.

At this point she heard the pony and retrieved the knife before shoving the barricade to one side and cracking open the door, carefully checking all angles before opening it wide.

Janey emerged slowly from the cottage and saw the pony.

'Good morning, handsome,' she whispered, distracted as she looked around warily.

Then she walked slowly and at some distance around the cottage holding the knife before her, crouched like some gypsy assassin. The pony joined her, following close behind.

When she stopped, he stopped.

'Some sort of ritual, is it?' said a man's voice from some distance behind her.

Janey shrieked, the knife went skywards and the pony ran off.

On the path along the cliffs stood Ross.

'Oh, I am sorry, Janey,' he called out. 'Didn't mean to startle you.'

Janey began to run towards him. 'I've been so frightened.' Then she stopped and shrieked again. 'You can't see me like this!'

She dashed towards the cottage, calling out: 'Wait there. I'll be with you in a minute.'

Ross shook his head, his expression showing mild amusement. He took in the view of the pony, which was now stopped some distance away and looking towards Ross and the cottage.

'You and me both,' said Ross, quietly, shaking his head. 'You and me both.'

Janey's head appeared from the cottage door. Then just her hand was visible. It is waving.

'Either she's indicating she and the cottage are about to turn right, or she wants me to go over,' Ross decided.

Ross entered, viewing the destruction with awe. Janey was sat, studying the contents of the biscuit tin.

'You really know how to live,' said Ross. 'Did anybody die?'

Janey looked up and handed the papers to Ross.

'I found these last night,' she said, ignoring his comment. 'They spilled from that biscuit tin which was on top of the closet. I didn't look at them at the time. They're not very nice.'

Ross flicked through the first few. There was a child's drawing, a pressed-flower, a simple photograph of a girl on a horse.

Then Ross's expression became grim, but he didn't speak. The photographs had grown less innocent and Ross stopped sifting through them, his expression hardening.

'There was a man here last night,' Janey added. 'Or rather, a man was looking through the window last night. I had to use bits of furniture to barricade the door.'

Ross replied, distractedly: 'Which kept him out.'

Janey nodded, then her expression turned to surprise. 'Did you hear what I said? There was a peeping Tom here last night. I was terrified.'

'Huh. Oh, sorry,' said Ross. 'Distracted. You're right, these are not very nice.'

Ross saw the biscuit tin on the floor, put the documents and photographs in and closed the lid firmly. Then he turned towards Janey, holding up the tin before placing it on the breakfast bar. 'Product of a sick mind, I think.' He looked around. 'Pack what you need and I'll help you carry it to the Grange. You're not staying here.'

Chapter Nine

In the porch of the Grange, Ross lowered several packages to the floor as Janey removed her backpack.

'I'm sorry to be a burden,' apologised Janey, again. 'I could still find a room somewhere.'

'Won't hear of it,' said Ross, firmly.

Mrs Armitage arrived, cleaning her hands on her apron.

'Mrs. Armitage. We have a guest,' he continued. 'Janey will be staying with us for a while.'

'Oh, good. Can I help you with your bags?'

Ross answered. 'No, but I hope your husband can.'

'I'll get him. Then I'll take you to your room.'

Ross hadn't finished: 'Perhaps we can have tea in the lounge when you come down, Janey.'

'Love to.'

Janey left as Mr and Mrs Armitage returned.

Janey and Ross were sat in the lounge, going through the contents of the biscuit tin.

'Hmm,' murmured Ross. 'We've not really got enough to go worrying the police with.'

'But.. The horrible photographs...,' Janey protested.

'I'd like to hold on to these for the moment,' he replied. 'They're connected with the case I told you about. The girl in the pictures is the same girl.'

'Oh! How terrible.'

Janey and Ross were quiet for a few moments.

'I definitely saw someone,' said Janey, eventually, her tone slightly affronted.

'Oh, I believe you,' said Ross, quickly, concerned. Then he relaxed. 'But don't you think we ought to weigh the pros and cons first?'

'Go on.'

Ross leant towards Janey. 'Well, let's see it from the police's perspective. Woman on her own, at night, in a cottage far from her neighbours. Likely to get a bit spooky, they'll say. Then they may ask why you are staying at the cottage.' Ross looked uncomfortable. 'You say you are convalescing. They immediately jump to the conclusion that you must have been hallucinating. Then they'll say it is your word....against persons unknown, because you haven't even got a description.'

'I sort of saw him but can't describe what I saw.'

'See what I mean?'

Janey was subdued. 'Unfortunately, yes,' she said, 'but it's difficult to take when you spent most of the night worrying. And then there's those pictures'

'As I say,' persisted Ross, 'I'd like you to hold onto them for the moment. They're evidence regarding what is, after all, an old story.' His tone became upbeat: 'As for me, I see this as a blessing in disguise.'

Janey looked at him questioningly.

Ross responded quickly. 'But for your suffering, that is.' He smiled. 'Your being out of that shabby cottage....even though you had customised it to your own peculiar architectural tastes, makes me a lot happier.'

Janey picked up a cushion and threatens to throw it at him. 'Cheek!'

Ross pretended to duck away from the potential missile. 'Careful with the furnishings. We have greater regard for them here than in some places.'

Janey smiled. Then she looked around the room. 'Who owns this?'

'Same person who owns your cottage. In fact, he owns about two thousand acres around here. Spends most of the year abroad. Rents most things out, through his solicitors. The bigger properties come with staff.' Ross bent forward conspiratorially. 'Probably to stop the tenants running off with the silver, says the cynic in me.'

'How long have you got it for?'

'I took it for six months. Been here two. With a bit of luck I'll have the book finished by the end of this let.'

Ross looked closely but kindly at Janey. 'Of course, there have been a few distractions, so I may have to extend.'

Janey rose and walked to the window. She looked out, and then turned to Ross. 'I feel safe here.'

Behind her, through the window in the garden, Mr Armitage was walking up the drive towards the house.

Sunny was playing on a swing. Nearby, Luke was sat on a bench with his mobile phone to his ear. 'We've got a problem,' he said, then paused as he listened to the response, before going on. 'Janey, of course. Listen, I got a call from the doctor's surgery. The blood test results are in and they want her to fix an appointment.' He paused. 'That's what I thought. Enough to sink a battleship.' He paused again. 'Yes, yes. I forget when David's back. He'll have to review them first…. Look, just calm down. All you've got to do is say you saw her taking tablets at her office. Right. Leave the rest to me. We'll bluff it out.'

Janey brushed away a tear and was embarrassed at her emotion.

'Just what are you convalescing from?' Ross's tone was gentle.

'You mean, what happened?'

Ross nodded. Then: 'If you don't want to tell me, that's fine.'

Janey was quiet for a few moments, eyes averted, but she raised them and looked straight into his eyes. 'I've been running the sharp end of an IT department for what seems an eternity. Used to be high-excitement - over-exciting at times. It took over my life, even my family. My child spent her first two years on my lap as I logged-in from home.' Janey pulled a face. 'Are you sure you want to hear this?'

Ross nodded. Janey's expression became reflective and her eyes looked away from him. 'Then it became work, which gradually became stress. I had a few events that I managed to cover up by taking leave or inventing excuses to be out of the office. But then, recently, something happened that I still don't understand. I really lost the plot.'

Janey recounted her last day at the office and brushed away a tear.

Ross had been watching her attentively. Then they were both silent for a few moments.

'I'm sure everything will turn out well,' reassured Ross. 'Will you be able to continue your painting here or do you have to go back again to the cliffs?'

'I'm working on the detail now,' replied Janey, her mood improving with the change of subject. 'Might need to go back to check the colours but I don't think so. I don't even need to be outside. Having said that, I wouldn't mind working on the painting out there.'

He followed her gaze as she looked in the direction of the window, and the terrace beyond. 'Though I might find the view from your terrace too distracting, ' she added, getting up and walking over to the window.

Ross rose and joined Janey at the window. He was standing close to her.

'It's certainly something, isn't it?'

Janey was affected, but not negatively, by his nearness. 'I'll get my things,' she said, moving away.

At the door she paused and turned back. 'Oh, just one thing. May I use your phone. I ought to let my family know where I am.'

A trace of disappointment flashed across Ross's face at the mention of others with a claim on Janey, but he instantly returned to the role of caring host.

'Of course. In the hall on the left,' he said, with a smile.

Janey was using the phone and keeping her voice low. Over her shoulder, Ross was casually watching through the open door of the lounge.

'No, I'm fine, Luke. Nothing to worry about. I'm staying at the Grange. A nice couple are looking after me.'

She paused to listen to Luke who was saying something about the frame he'd given her. At first she didn't understand but then remembered the object he'd tried to force upon her and which she'd later found on the grass by the helicopter landing place. She didn't want to talk about it so cut him off. 'It's going well,' she said.

'Are you sure, he asked,' concern in his voice.

'Yes, really. Look, this is not my phone. I'll call you when I can. Love to Sunny.'

At dinner, Janey and Ross were sat at opposite ends of a large, formal, table. They were chatting politely, their body language suggested they were still strangers.

Following the meal they returned to the lounge were they took coffee and Ross offered liqueurs. Janey turned down the latter but Ross went ahead with his. 'It's a reward,' he said, as he put his drink on the coffee table, 'for working so hard.'

Something in Janey's expression prompted Ross to say: 'What is it?'

'I've just remembered something,' she replied. 'I'll need some more bits from the cottage.'

'Why don't *we* pick them up tomorrow?' he offered. 'I don't like the thought of you going back there alone.'

'Better still,' she suggested, 'we could do the walk you were doing when I first met you.'

'Good idea. A ten mile hike will be just the ticket.

Janey looked at him disapprovingly.

'Five miles?' he suggested.

She nodded. 'A five mile walk, avoiding the direct route through hedgerows and swamps. Now that's more like it.'

Janey woke at three in the morning, suddenly wide awake. She had no idea why this should be but, without hesitation, she dragged out the sketchpad and started to do some more work for the picture, which stood propped up against the wall in its semi-finished state.

While doing this she found herself going over the telephone call with Luke earlier. She wondered why she hadn't told him about Ross. Was it guilt?

She also tried to remember what else he had been talking about. Then she remembered: it was about the frame.

Pausing in her work she went over to where her parka was draped over a chair and retrieved the frame from a pocket.

It was really just a picture frame with a stand at the back just like any other. Perhaps Luke had wanted her to place it somewhere where she could always look at it. But it wasn't displaying a photograph now. Instead, it seemed to her to be a list of symptoms which characterised a nervous breakdown. As soon as she saw the term 'nervous breakdown' she dropped the frame on the bed as if it was electrified and returned to her sketching.

The sketching was coming on now and she was finally managing to capture the spontaneity of the spume flying off the waves as they crashed against the rocks at the base of the cliffs. Even the rollers behind had a feel to them as they seemed to break over the reefs. The momentary slack water appeared to carry the veined water collecting white and various greys like a skin which climbed like a wall on the back of the next roller.

Having got the sketch down on paper she would later transfer the effect to the painting and use it as a structure for applying the oils.

Such sketch work was tiring. The attention to detail made her eyes hurt and she could only concentrate for short periods. So it was, only minutes later, she decided to take a break from her work.

Remembering the frame again, she scooped it up and began to read its contents.

Approaching a psychotic event: the warning signs.

When a nervous breakdown's near,
 some symptoms of it may be clear.
Not every symptom will be there -
 that's just impossible, to be fair.
But knowing what your symptoms are for sure,
 will help you on the road to a cure.
What are these signs you say, I hear,
 well let me tell them to you, dear:

> **P**aranoid that people mean you harm
> **A**ppetite for food – too little or too much
> **S**leep disturbed or too much
> **S**eeing people who are not there
> **A**nxiety attacks
> an**G**er without provocation
> h**E**aring voices
> **S**uicidal thoughts
>
> **A**lcohol or drug abuse
> **F**lashbacks to traumatic events
> formal **R**elationships become difficult or impossible
> **A**lienation of family and friends
> feeling **I**nvincible or of grandeur
> **D**isinterest in work or family life

So now you have a useful crib,
 there's no need for your usual *ad lib*.
Just know what's real and a not at all zany,
 and bring us back our precious Janey (and Mummy).

LUKE (and Sunny)

As she read through the list she found herself ticking off the symptoms she had experienced recently and it began to explain things. She really *was* imagining things, it seemed to be telling her. Her paranoia at the cottage was explained in the symptoms. She *had* imagined the face at the window. She really was ill. Even her sleeplessness was a symptom.

It said something for her state of mind that she did not respond normally to Luke's attempt at humour in posting this serious message. Even when she read his name, and that of her daughter, she felt herself wanting to keep them out of her mind. Again, she didn't know why. At least, she wouldn't admit to herself why she might be feeling this way.

But there was some reaction. For a while she felt quite depressed and then decided it was all rubbish and didn't apply to her. Within minutes she had decided once more to ignore it and its wisdom. She knew best, she told herself. It was all poppycock, she decided, exhibiting another one of the symptoms. 'Well,' she said. 'I'll go to sleep and end my conformance to another symptom - sleep disruption or too much sleep.'

She replaced the photograph frame in the pocket of her parka, pushed the sketch materials onto the floor, returned to bed and was asleep in moments – and she slept until almost ten a.m.

Janey and Ross crossed a stile. It was just after eleven in the morning and the sky was clear. He helped her over and they laughed at her awkwardness. As they walked on, Ross pointed out various landmarks and Janey showed increasing interest as she looked at the view.

At one point she gasped at the scenery, the rolling moors and the rugged cliffs and windswept sea beyond, and remembered the happy days when she and Luke had back-packed their way along this coast in their first summer. It seemed an age ago now but she remembered it with fondness. She almost said that Luke would enjoy the view but stopped herself. She didn't know why. Was it guilt? Why? She hadn't done anything wrong, had she? She couldn't see what the problem was in her confused state and so let it go.

Ross was still talking. He seemed to know a lot about the area, including the flora. When Janey paused to look back across the moors she couldn't help mentioning the bleakness.

'Not a bit of it,' responded Ross. 'The place is absolutely teeming with stuff. Admittedly there is a lot of heather and gorse about the place …'

'And bog,' she interrupted.

'And bog,' he agreed, 'but a lot of other stuff doesn't just provide greenery it's quite useful medicinally as well. Take Butcher's Broom for instance….'

Janey was smiling.

Ross stopped. Then: 'You're laughing at me.'

'No,' said Janey, slowly. 'It's nice to hear you feel so passionately about this place.'

'It shows, does it?'

'A tad, perhaps.'

They laughed.

'I told you I could be a bit pompous. Now I'm also revealing that I'm a bore,' he said. 'What shall I impress you with next?'

Eventually, they arrived at the coast some distance along the cliffs from where the cottage was located. The sea was fairly rough and there was a cold breeze blowing. Both were glad to be well wrapped up.

The scene ahead was indeed beautiful, it seemed to Janey, but she realised her view might have been influenced by the company. It occurred to her that they were getting along very well.

Then, as they approached the cottage Janey's feelings changed and she was suddenly quiet. Ross picked up on the mood change and knew the reason. 'If you like I can go in and get what you want,' he offered.

'No,' she said, firmly. 'I think I prefer to get my undies myself.'

Taking this as a warning to stay outside, Ross stayed by the cliff edge but kept a keen eye on the cottage.

As it was, Janey was in and out of the cottage in no time.

'Would you like to go down to the beach?' he asked.

'Excellent idea,' she responded. 'We could go down by George and Margaret's cottage, the cliffs are almost down to sea-level there. I saw them when I went to ask for help with the roof. There's even a track of sorts.'

Ross frowned. 'Not a good idea,' he decided. 'Let's go the other way. It'll be a bit more difficult getting down to the beach but I won't tarnish your reputation that way.'

'What?'

He smiled. '"What," she says.'

She giggled.

'And what a nice noise you make when you laugh. Like breaking glass.'

'A bit forward, aren't you,' she said, her tone mock admonishment. 'But what's the problem with going that way,' she added.

Ross frowned again, his expression suddenly dark. 'We, George and I don't get on. If that isn't an under-statement. If he sees you with me - a likely event as we'll need to pass within a few feet of the cottage - he'll associate you with being in cahoots with me. If he then sees us going down to the beach...'

'He'll think we're going over his daughter's death,' she interrupted. 'Okay, let's go this way,' she added, grabbing his arm and encouraging him to move off the other way.

Getting down to the beach was accomplished at the lowest point in the cliff along the coast to the right of Janey's cottage. Even though it was no more than fifty feet from cliff-top to sea-level, finding footholds was sometimes not straightforward and several times Ross helped Janey navigate the more difficult places.

In truth, she didn't need help but she responded to his gallantry and enjoyed the physical contact on their short trip to the beach.

Down on the shoreline the sea was quite mild and the waves splashed harmlessly a safe distance away from where they stood at the bottom of the cliff face. The beach was far from perfect, with the small areas of sand segregated by rocks in slab or sharks' teeth form that although unusual, produced an attractive scene.

Although Janey was enjoying herself, especially paddling where she could along the shoreline among the wavelets, she could see that Ross was distracted. She tried to keep the banter going but he was not participating. They had been making their way slowly back in the direction of the cottage for some time but, chattering away, she only realised belatedly that he had been steering her inland towards the cliff and away from the shore, keeping the other cottage out of sight all the time.

Janey decided it wasn't wise to broach the subject of the girl's death and the problem between Ross and George, but she was intrigued at Ross's concern.

She looked up as they reached the headland just below where 'her' cottage was located and experienced a frisson of fear.

Distracted though he had been, Ross picked up on her reaction, principally because she had stopped talking. 'What is it?' he asked, concerned.

'This cliff,' she said, looking up. 'It's where I was painting that first day. I lost most of my paint stuff when it blew away. I decided to go after it and started to climb down the cliff.'

'You tried to climb down that!'

Above them the cliff was undercut from about fifty feet over their heads, starting just feet below where Janey had clung, shaking, on that first day. Both automatically let their gaze drop to the debris field beneath it. There were no remnants of her painting things on the 'beach' but there were many jagged boulders which, in their eyes, no longer formed the pretty scenery they had once thought.

In her mind's eye she saw her lifeless body draped across one of the rocks. 'Well, that would certainly have sorted out my problems,' she said, reflectively.

'Let's go,' said Ross, and they moved back the way they had come.

On top of the cliff they walked straight inland. As they continued on their way, the mood returned to its early good humour and, from time to time, she looked around but there was no sign of the pony.

They fell quiet for a while, but it appeared to be too much for Ross. 'Is this helping?' He waved a hand at the surroundings.

Janey turned to look in the direction he had indicated. The moor was there but they now saw the pastureland that surrounded the Grange ahead of them. 'It is a special place,' she confirmed. 'It makes me want to stop running.'

'Running?'

Janey laughed. 'Me, me, me. I don't know any-thing about you,' she said, accusingly.

'Me. I'm an open book. But what is this running thing?'

Janey was suddenly serious. 'I seem to have been running all my life. Do well at school, get a good job, marry, have a child before it is too late, work, work, work.'

'Who's applying the pressure to keep running?'

'Me, of course. I just can't stop working. The tread-mill is my life and I can't get off. I'm not enjoying it but I can't get off.' The realisation seemed to shock her.

'But this...here...is helping?'

Janey smiled. 'Oh, yes. Very much so. But part of me wonders why I'm delaying getting back onto the treadmill.'

'Guilt?'

'That's exactly it. Guilt.' She shook her head. 'But the thing is...I don't know why I'm feeling guilty.'

Ross noted the hopelessness in her eyes. She was trapped and needed to get out.

'I'm sure the rest here will sort it out. Give it a month-or-so and you'll wonder what a treadmill is, never mind how to get on one.'

'Wouldn't that be great. But there's no way I can stay away for a month or anywhere near... I have to get back.'

'To the treadmill?'

'Yes, you're right. I need to relax—at least a little bit longer. I know I'm not ready to go back yet. I still feel strange.'

'How strange? No, I mean how do you feel strange?'

'Too many things to list,' she said, irritated, but her irritation was with herself. 'For instance, I keep forgetting things in mid-sentence and I've still a lot of anger against the company I work for.'

Ross shrugged. 'We all forget things, Janey. Nothing strange there. Sometimes I find if I've a lot to think about at the same time—or I'm under pressure—I can instantly forget what I'm saying or doing. You can't plead being different on that score.'

He smiled. 'As for the anger. Who hasn't felt anger against their job or the people in it. Anyone in particular.'

Janey's tone was exasperated. 'Yes, but I get angry at the least provocation. I lead ...' she was about say Luke, but changed her mind. She saved her embarrassment by saying. 'There you go, I forgot what I was going to say again.'

'You lead something,' cued Ross.

'I lead people dogs' lives,' she continued, 'if that makes sense. And I know I'm doing it but can't help it.'

'Who in particular has angered you?'

'There's this one man, Steve. Works for me. He's let me down too often,' she said, her expression hardening.

'You associate him with failure, perhaps? You don't think that he may not be the man for the particular job, or your difficulties are preventing you from using him effectively?'

'Wow! You're not pulling any punches, are you?'

Ross smiled. 'Hey, take it easy. We're out on a walk on a beautiful—if cold—day and I'm an amateur psychiatrist who's trying to put the other side of the argument, that's all.'

'So there's nothing wrong with me,' she said, a little annoyed. Standing with her hands on her hips.

Ross grinned. 'Not from where I'm standing,' he said.

In response, Janey managed to laugh.

They walked on and soon they were walking back along the drive to the Grange and lunch.

In the afternoon, Janey moved her painting stuff out onto the terrace. It was while she was working here that she found her mind wandering back to the walk. She felt she was really beginning to relax now, she told herself. She found Ross to be kind and responsive to her mild flirting, and she felt that a little flirting wouldn't hurt one bit.

Occasionally she looked back to the Grange and once saw Ross looking at her through a downstairs window. He was sat at a computer. He waved.

Janey changed for dinner and made a special effort to control her errant hair and appear a little more girly.

By some magic of organisation, Janey and Ross this evening were sat at one end of the table, on opposite sides, having dinner. They chatted informally, diffidence having disappeared from their manner. Their body language had become that of friends.

'It's a funny thing, mental illness,' said Ross, once they'd re-located to the lounge.

'Not that funny,' she responded.

'Point taken,' he said, slightly embarrassed. 'Perhaps, odd would be a better word.'

'How do you mean?'

'It's so difficult to describe compared with physical illness even though I see what you're getting at when you talk about it.'

Janey didn't help by looking blankly at him.

Ross sighed, then shrugged. 'Oh, I don't know what I'm trying to say, either.' Then: 'Yes, I do.'

He sat down in the easy chair and leant forward towards Janey, who was almost reclining on the settee.

'For many years I had a back problem,' he said. 'I'd been doing a lot of manual labour during my gap year and during the holidays. Little tweaks when lifting things were ignored and accommodated by a change in posture.'

He checked to see if Janey was still awake and got the 'And…' expression from her.

'Well, to cut a long story short, I went to see an osteopath when mild painkillers and exercise failed to fix the latest injury, a pulled ligament.' He snorted.

'Truth was I couldn't walk so an appointment with the medical fraternity was unavoidable.'

Ross got to his feet. 'Oh, I'm sorry. Did you want a drink?'

Janey picked up her wine-glass which was still fairly full. 'I think I can manage with this for the time being.'

'The osteopath told me that my spine was like a story, a list of injuries that were connected,' said Ross, pouring himself a brandy. 'Seems the vertebrae were arranged in a zig-zag, which is unusual.'

'A zig-zag,' responded Janey, feigning interest.

'Perhaps a slight exaggeration,' he amended hurriedly. 'Out of alignment, anyway. He told me that the first injury was at the right side of the base of my spine. I'd responded by changing my posture to alleviate the pain on the left that this caused. Then I'd changed my posture again to alleviate the discomfort caused by this further posture change and compounded the situation by my latest injury. Apparently my head was leaning to one side and I hadn't noticed it.'

'Are you alright now?'

'Yes, as it happens. He spent a considerable time treating each injury once he'd reduced the pain from the pulled ligament. Now it is as straight as it ever will be. But the point was that my spine had become twisted over time so that I couldn't function correctly and – in trying to alleviate the pain from the latest injury – I was causing more problems.'

'Instead of returning to the root cause and treating that?'

'Exactly. The relevance to mental illness is that so much of the problem is hidden – behind more recent problems which, in turn, cause their own problems.'

Janey appeared unconvinced.

'Just a thought,' added Ross. 'Trying to apply a bit of logic to things.'

'I think I see what you mean,' she responded. 'What doesn't kill you makes you stronger, perhaps, but there's a half-way-house where something doesn't actually kill you but weakens you in some way.'

'Right again,' he said, enthusiastically. 'You *have* got it.'

'Perhaps,' she corrected him. 'It's still a bit too complicated and deep for me after the wine.'

At eleven o'clock Janey excused herself and went up to bed, while Ross remained in the lounge nursing a glass. The wine had flowed somewhat and Janey had felt her nose going numb. Whether the wine was conspiring with the pills she'd taken she wasn't sure, but the numbness was a sign for her to go to bed. Once there she didn't bother to strip off. She nose-dived onto the bed and was asleep almost instantly.

The rattle would not go away. Try as she did to ignore whatever it was, it continued. She found she couldn't move. Her arms were tightly bound around her body and only her head was free. She looked around for the cause of the sound and why she was tied up. Then she dimly discerned a figure moving around her room, and a tiny pointer of light moved over her belongings stacked untidily on the floor next to the dresser. The drawers of the dresser were open slightly and one drawer pull was still swinging against the drawer. At the sight of the figure she screamed. She screamed as loud as she could but only the slightest murmur came out, though it was strangled almost at birth.

At the noise the figure turned round briefly but in the darkness it was impossible to see who it was. Then the figure moved over to the open window and exited with difficulty, banging something which caused an anguished groan to be emitted. Then the figure was through and closing the window, before disappearing completely.

At last her attempts to scream bore expression and the noise she made brought the people of the household to her door in short order. When she hadn't replied to their knock or calling her name, they entered and turned on the light.

On the bed, Janey was still struggling to rid herself of her bonds, rolling herself side to side, but to no avail.

Ross was in the lead, accompanied by Mrs Armitage and, in short order, by a muttering Mr Armitage, who was still dressing.

'Janey!' said Ross, alarmed. 'What is it?

'He went through the window. Hurry!' she said, still struggling.

Ross looked to the window then back to Janey.

'Who?'

'The burglar. There was someone in my room.'

'Here? Are you sure?'

'Yes, Ross. I'm sure,' she responded heatedly.

Armitage went over to the window and after a brief look through into the night, looked up to the sash-lock and put his hand on it. 'This is locked,' he announced. Then he moved back and leaned on the dresser, his expression unimpressed.

'But I saw him. He must have tied me up and ....' Janey halted as she realised what Mr Armitage had said.

Ross looked down at her, a quizzical expression on his face. 'Tied you up? How?'

She looked down, now with the benefit of light. There were no bonds, just the bedclothes which were wrapped around her quite tightly.

Janey began to cry with frustration. 'Will someone please get me out of this?'

Mrs Armitage managed to extricate Janey from the bedclothes with difficulty. It had required that Janey roll along the bed as one would to free someone wrapped in a carpet. Given her emotional state this was not easy but eventually she was revealed in the same clothes she had worn at dinner. She sat up.

Ross was quiet through this. Then he looked around. 'Is anything missing?' he asked.

Janey looked around. 'I don't know,' she said. 'The drawers are open, but I don't think I put anything in there.'

The others looked at the mess of belongings on the floor but made no comment.

Ross went over to the drawer. 'Which drawer is open? All these are shut.'

Janey leaned forward to peer at the dresser. 'They *were* open. It was the noise of the handles rattling that woke me up.'

Ross shrugged. The drawers were closed so there was nothing he could add.

He looked to Mrs Armitage and Mr Armitage, who were looking to him for guidance. He had his back to Janey and she didn't see his look. It was pretty clear to the couple that he didn't believe Janey.

'I think I can cope here,' said Ross. 'Perhaps you could have a look around outside, Mr Armitage?'

Mr Armitage nodded and left, followed by his wife.

Ross went over to the bed and sat down, next to Janey. 'Are you okay now?' he asked.

Janey tried to smile. 'Yes, I think so.'

'We didn't drink much last night but I should have known you would also be taking tablets.' He smiled. 'You don't think they may have affected you in some way?'

When she spoke, Janey's tone was belligerent. 'What do you mean?' I felt a bit tipsy but I wasn't drunk. I came up to my room and went to bed, that's all'

'That's not what I'm saying, Janey,' he protested, mildly. 'I'm merely suggesting that the drink and the tablets conspired and…you probably had a nightmare?'

'I imagined it all. That's what you're saying.' She thought about this for a moment, shocked. 'No!' he was here, I saw him.'

'Him?'

Janey looked uncomfortable. 'Well, I can't be sure it was a *him, a 'he'*, but there was someone here. I'm sure of it.'

'Sure? You weren't actually tied up, were you?'

Janey shrugged and looked down at the bed.

'Mr Armitage checked the window and it was locked,' continued Ross.

Janey winced. 'I can't understand that.' Her expression was confused. 'It doesn't make sense.'

'I checked the drawers and they were all shut,' he added.

'I don't understand,' she said. 'I couldn't have just imagined it.' She looked at him imploringly.

'Want to know what I think?' he said.

She nodded, mute.

'You *did* have a nightmare…'

'But I saw...'

'Hear me out,' he said firmly, but waited for Janey to return to a less excited state before continuing. 'You were 'drugged' last evening with the combination of wine and tablets. It's partly my fault. As I say, I should have realised you were on medication.'

He shook his head, irritated with himself. 'Nevertheless, when you came to bed you fell asleep on top of the bed. Later, when you grew cold, you wrapped the bedclothes around you. Being 'out of it' you probably didn't realise that you were, in effect, wrapping yourself up like a mummy.

'Then you had your dream, which you tried to participate in but found you were 'bound' and couldn't move. You probably panicked and the dream – perhaps a version of your fright at the cottage – merged into each other and you woke up.'

'I tried and tried but I couldn't scream,' she said. 'Nothing would come out.'

'Oh, you could scream alright – not at first, when you were in the middle of your nightmare – but the hounds of the Baskervilles could learn something from you,' he returned, smiling.

Janey didn't say anything but she nodded almost imperceptibly.

'Do you want anything,' he asked.

'A stiff drink?' she suggested

Ross raised an eyebrow. 'Perhaps not. I was thinking more along the lines of a cup of tea.'

'No. I think I'm okay.'

Ross went around to the windows and made a show of checking they were locked. Then he went over to the bathroom and checked in there. He also checked the wardrobe and finally, under the bed.

'Point taken,' she said, as he looked up from this last action. 'I'll be alright now. I'm sorry to be such a nuisance.'

Ross smiled. 'It's not a big problem, Janey.' He moved over to the bed again. 'You had a nightmare and that you did is absolutely no surprise to me after what you've been through. I just hope you can get some sleep now.'

'Thank you, Ross,' she said. 'I'll be a good little girl now.'

'Well, perhaps a quieter one,' he suggested.

They heard a knock then and Mr Armitage put his head around the door. He looked over to Ross and shook his head. 'No sign of anything out there,' he said.

Ross nodded and Mr Armitage departed.

'So it was all just a dream,' said Janey, beginning at last to relax.

Ross got up and moved to the door. 'Now that you know there are no bogeymen in your room. Why don't you use this,' he tapped the key in the lock, 'it's what it's there for and you'll feel safer. Good night.'

Chapter Ten

The following morning, after breakfast, Janey and Ross were to be found tacking up the pony. They had not discussed the events of the early morning, both were just happy to consign the incident to the past.

Now Janey admired her handiwork. 'I knew it would fit,' she said, triumphantly. Then she turned to Ross. 'This is no coincidence. This tack belongs to the pony. I suspected as much when I saw the girl on the pony in the photograph. This confirms it.'

'But why would it be here?' Ross was clearly confused. Then: 'Mr Armitage will know.' He looked about him. 'I'll go and find him.'

Ross departed for the house.

While he was gone, Janey busied herself with adjusting the tack, flexing the pony's legs and tightening the girth straps.

Ross returned. 'That's that mystery cleared up,' he said. 'Armitage tells me the owner bought the pony and tack off the Smiths following the tragedy. He'd some notion of using it for his children but more likely, according to the Armitages, it was to help the Smiths at a critical time. Armitage has been cleaning the tack regularly since as one of his duties. The owner told him to release the pony rather than feed him every day. The entire property is fenced so he can't go anywhere. I also found out Armitage is awaiting further instructions from the owner.'

'So that's it. You get the impression the owner knows as much about horses as you do.'

Ross showed mock indignation. 'Thank you very much!'

Janey smiled, apologetically. 'No offence. Giving the pony its freedom is one thing but horses and ponies are social animals. They need company. There're few worse sights in the countryside than the view of a solitary horse standing alone in a paddock for days on end without company or daily visits from people.'

'Surely that is tautology.'

'*Touché*, Mr Writer.'

'Actually, I'm wrong,' decided Janey.

'Wrong? A woman? Wrong?' Ross appeared to be savouring the words like a rare wine.

Janey ignored him. 'An old horse that loses its companion is sometimes best left alone because it might be bullied if it was made to share with a younger horse.'

'You really do know your stuff,' said Ross, admiringly.

'I used to, a long time ago,' she said, feeling awkward. 'A very long time ago.'

For once the sky was blue and although still cold they were keeping warm as they moved on along the country lane. Janey was riding the pony and after trotting on ahead from Ross, chastised him for not keeping up.

Although he remonstrated with her for this his and her moods were light and playful. They were enjoying the day out and it wasn't just because of the improvement in the weather, although that was a consideration. The weak sun was beginning to burn off the light mist.

Eventually they came across a pub which had a few tables outside.

'I think that's enough toil for the moment,' said Ross, slightly out of breath. 'Time for a pit-stop. Pull up a hitching rail, or whatever you horsey people say.'

Janey giggled. Then she slid off the pony in an accomplished dismount.

While Janey found a table inside the pub, Ross went to pick up some drinks from the bar. Once there he was distracted by a leaflet on top of a pile of such documents stacked untidily on the bar. 'Local Show' it announced and bore a drawing of a horse.

Back at the table with their drinks, Ross dropped the leaflet onto the table and nudged Janey. 'It's tomorrow. What do you think?'

Janey picked up the leaflet. 'You're joking. Me?'

'Don't see why not. You've ridden before,' justified Ross. 'Let's have a look at it.'

When Janey didn't respond he glanced over to her. He noticed she was casting an eye around the gloomy interior. There were other people at other tables but no-one she recognised.

'Do you want to move,' asked Ross.

'No, this is fine. I'm a mess.'

'S'funny how women always worry about their appearance more in public when other women are around,' said Ross.

Janey laughed. 'You sure you're not a psychiatrist?'

Ross tapped his head. 'It's the observant mind of a crime writer. Anyway, you mean psychologist - a psychiatrist treats people.'

'We're pretty huffy, aren't we? I'd have thought…' Janey's voice faded as she felt the presence of someone at her side. The figure carried a deerstalker hat.'

It was Ross who spoke. 'Well, if it isn't George Smith.'

George ignored Ross. 'Hello, Janey. The builder rang and he can't make it until next week. I made the mistake of telling him we'd patched it up. You've slipped down his priorities list, I'm afraid. He wants to know if you want to try somewhere else or stick with him.'

Janey was a little flustered. 'Oh, er. Thank you. I think we'll leave it with him. Thank you for letting me know.'

'Fine,' said George, who then looked at Ross with disapproval. 'Some queer company you keep.'

Ross rose to face George, fists clenched.

Margaret appeared behind George and pulled at his arm. 'George! Let's go.'

George moved away to their table. Meanwhile, Ross went to the door and left the pub.

Margaret turned to Janey. 'Sorry about that, Janey. The pair of them seem to be at each other's throats. I've no idea why… but it really worries me.'

Janey smiled, weakly.

The pony was grazing and Ross was standing nearby and facing away from the pub when Janey saw them.

Janey approached with the drinks and put them on a table. She was nervous. She hesitated to approach Ross. Then she noticed the leaflet still in her hand and walked up to him.

'I suppose I could try one of the smaller classes,' she said. 'Three foot or something. I've no idea how good the pony is but I'm sure he's competed before.'

Ross turned and smiled weakly. 'Sorry about that in there.'

Janey smiled.

Ross's mood changed, suddenly he was enthusiastic. 'Bloody good idea. Let's win some silverware.'

'Hold on there,' protested Janey. 'This isn't Hickstead.'

Ross moved over to the table with Janey and they sat down.

'It's probably none of my business but what was that all about with George?'

Ross made a face. 'You deserve some sort of explanation, I suppose,' admitted Ross. Then he sighed, loudly. 'I told you I've been researching this… ,' he looked around and then moved forward conspiratorially, 'death. It seems my digging around has come to the notice of the girl's father. Correction, adoptive father. The girl was an orphan when they took her in at the age of seven. Mrs Smith seemed sympathetic to my enquiries but he has been against me from the start.'

'Could it be that he is still feeling her loss and would like to move on without your reminding him?'

Ross's face grew hard but then softened. 'Two, no, three things we learn today,' he said, smiling. 'Janey Holland is on the mend; Janey Holland's logic is sound, and; her constant, very welcome, distractions have prevented me studying more closely the contents of the box you found, a task I will undertake at my earliest convenience. Bring me my steed. Er, Shall we go?'

They were both a bit tipsy on the beer and each other as they walked down the track. They were larking about as they walked along, this time with Ross on the pony.

They were closer now and they formed a tight group with the pony.

A flicker of seriousness flickered across Ross's face. 'What if he suddenly runs out of control?'

'You mean: what do you do if he bolts?'

Ross nodded.

'Stay with him. Don't try and bale out. You'll kill yourself. Try to turn him in circles, gradually reducing the radius. He'll stop rather than fall over.'

Ross did not appear to be encouraged by this bit of advice. 'I'll try to maintain the presence of mind that goes with that vision. The fact that we could end up in the next county. Lost. The blind leading the nearly blind-drunk...'

'You should have no worries on that score. Once he's calmed down he'll probably take you home.'

Ross was sceptical. 'Really?'

'They usually do,' confirmed Janey. 'They have an uncanny knack of knowing where they live - and always know how to find their way back to it. Generally by the shortest route.' She paused, her expression mischievous. 'Over fences. Across motorways. Through swamps.'

'Hmm, your attempts to make me feel more comfortable are not working,' murmured Ross. 'Give me a hand off this thing. Things could get tricky.'

'Not with me holding the pony on a lead-rope,' reminded Janey, smugly, shortening up on the rope so that she held it just below its attachment to the bridle while Ross dismounted in an ungainly fashion.

They were laughing as they walked into the stable yard, where they hitched the pony.

Janey spoke to the pony. 'How would you like a wash and brush-up?' She pretended to listen for a moment. 'Thought you would.'

'I think this is my cue to slope off and inquire about dinner,' offered Ross.

'Wimp!'

Ross left.

Janey brought a water-bucket to the pony.

She watched as it ignored the water.

Janey put the bucket down and turned away. 'In your own time.'

Over the best part of an hour Janey busied herself with grooming the pony. First she knocked off the worst of the dirt with brushes. Then she hosed him down and lathered him up, before rinsing him off, Then she scraped off the excess water from him with a squeegee. Finally, she brushed out his mane and tail.

'Spotless,' she decided, admiring him as he slept, his stifle locked into position. 'I think you enjoyed that and it didn't do me any harm either.'

Ross returned.

'Just in time,' said Janey. 'I've finished.'

'Never underestimate the value of timing,' advised Ross. Then he looked at Janey's muddied features and clothes. 'So this is what a wash and brush up does to you.'

'It's called grooming,' she corrected. 'It's a technical term, which, loosely translated for the uninitiated, means transferring the dirt from the horse to yourself.'

At the sound of conversation the pony stirred and after stretching out its previously raised foot, stood square on all four feet.

'What do we do with him now?' Ross clearly had no clue. 'This,' said Janey. She then removed the head

-collar and let him go with a gentle pat on his shoulder.

The pony drifted away to the nearest area of grass.

Janey was watching the pony closely. 'The observant writer,' she said, in the voice of a haughty headmistress, 'will note the horse's behaviour at this juncture. Following turn out after hosing down and lengthy grooming the horse will almost immediately …' Janey waited, the horses legs buckled and it descended to the ground where it started rocking. '… roll. Thus undoing a great deal of the effort put in by the groom!'

The pony returned to its feet, shook his self violently, and returned his head to the grazing position.

'Time for a bath,' announced Janey.

Janey and Ross walked back to the house.

'Tell me?' he said. 'How do *grooms* roll after a bath?'

In response, Janey elbowed him playfully in the side.

Janey and Ross were sat at a corner of the dinner table. Janey was looking a little tipsy, and was slurring her words.

'Shall we retire to the lounge?' asks Ross.

'Why not? Let's get more comfortable.'

Ross rose from his chair. 'I'd offer you a liqueur but I think we may have had enough.'

Janey grabbed the wine-bottle. 'Besides, we don't need liqueurs, we already have the grape.'

Janey filled her glass to the point where it over-flowed. 'Oops.' Hastily she sipped some wine away while the glass was still on the table.

'Let me carry it through for you,' offered Ross.

Janey smiled vacuously. 'Thank you, kind slur.'

Janey wobbled slightly on her way to the lounge where she flung herself back on the settee before awkwardly regaining a sitting position.

Ross brought their wine in and cast his eye around for somewhere to sit.

Janey patted the cushion beside her. 'Come and sit by me, Ross.'

Ross, warily, obliged.

Janey sighed dreamily. 'I've had a wonderful day.'

'I'm glad. So have I. Truly wonderful.'

'And you're a wonderful man,' slurred Janey. 'So courteous. But…' She struggled to find the words but then, her expression turned grave. '…flawed. Serious-ly flawed.'

'Oh, how?'

'Because you're a real gentleman,' explained Janey.

'And that's a flaw?'

Janey nodded, her expression still serious. 'Yes. Mr Perfect, it's a flaw, and I'll tell you why it's a flaw.'

Ross looked at her expectantly.

'Because you haven't made a pass at me yet.' She looked glum. 'You think I'm ugly. You haven't even tried to kiss me.'

'Okay, I'll kiss you.'

Janey wiped her lips extravagantly. 'Oh, good, a real slapperooney.'

'A wha…'

Janey grabbed him and kissed him full on the mouth. It carried on for a while.

When she withdrew, Janey smiled inanely. 'That was very nice.'

Ross looked to the door.

In the voice of someone reasoning with a small child Ross says: 'I'd better let Mrs Armitage go if we're to repeat that.'

Janey looked confused for a moment. Then: 'Oh, yes.' She put her finger to her lips. 'Shh.'

Ross left the room. When he returned less than five minutes later Janey was asleep.

Ross smiled and moved the door wide open.

Then he moved over to Janey and looked at her for some moments to confirm she was asleep. He picked her up and carried her up the stairs.

As he reached the landing he heard a door shut along the corridor where Mr and Mrs Armitage's room is located.

Ross showed no sign of noticing but as he went past the door he knocked quietly. The door opened a little and Mrs Armitage looked out, dressed in a night gown.

Ross, mouthing the words without the sound, said: 'I need your help. Come with me.'

Ross took Janey to her bed and gently put her down.

Quietly, he said: 'I'll leave the rest to you.'

Mrs Armitage moved around the bed to attend to Janey, as Ross left the room.

Chapter Eleven

Ross was sat at the breakfast table, reading a newspaper. The debris of his breakfast was on the table and an untouched setting for Janey was on the other side.

Mrs Armitage put her head around the corner of the door and looked inquiringly at Ross.

Ross shrugged: 'Still no sign.'

Mrs Armitage retreated.

A moment later Ross heard footsteps and Janey appeared.

She was wearing sunglasses and appeared pale and unsteady.

Silently she took her seat.

Mrs Armitage re-entered the room.

'What would you like, madam?' She smiled. 'We have …'

Janey avoided eye contact. 'Nothing..to..eat, thank you. I'll just have some coffee.'

Ross smiled. 'Good morning.'

Janey finally looked up, her expression frail.

'I think we should go for a walk this morning, ' suggested Ross, looking at his watch. 'Er, afternoon.'

Janey did not stir. 'It's not even nine-thirty yet,' she corrected him, huffily, but her sagging shoulders seemed to indicate that it was still far too early for her.

By ten-thirty Janey and Ross were out walking and scanning the horizons.

'He's got to be somewhere,' complained Janey. 'You'd have thought we'd have seen him by now.' Then: 'God only knows why I agreed to this but we've got to be at the show at least an hour before for me to scrounge some riding kit.'

Ross was relaxed. 'He's a free agent. He can go wherever he likes. He's probably visiting some friends along the coast.'

'Go on, make fun of me.'

Relaxed as he was, Ross was still pushing the walking pace.

'Is this a route march?' enquired Janey.

'Sorry. I was in a world of my own. I tend to crack on when I'm not distracted.'

'Charming!' exclaimed Janey. 'Some distraction I turned out to be.'

'I thought you'd like a bit of time to come round. We put away quite a lot of wine last night,' he said, smiling. 'You fell asleep and I had to take you to bed.'

Janey looked at him pointedly but there was also an air of nervousness about her.

Ross pretended not to notice but walked on a few steps before speaking again. 'I did the carrying and Mrs. Armitage did the rest,' he said, offhandedly.

Janey swiped him with her hand on his arm. 'Swine.'

Ross laughed. 'How're you feeling?'

Janey groaned. 'Beyond a slight throbbing behind the eyes I feel fine. I'm beginning to feel really relaxed and ready for work again.'

'Proves the saying then,' said Ross, upbeat.

'What's that?'

'All work and no play makes Janey a dull boy.'

Janey stopped and faced him, hands on hips. 'Thank you very much. Is that how you see me - as a boy?'

'Of course not,' he responded, contrite. 'You know I don't. It's just a saying, but the truth is you didn't just need a rest, you needed a change.'

Janey stretched and sighed, then frowned and touched her head. 'You're right. I'm doing a lot of the things I thought I'd forgotten how to do. I feel alive. I feel I'm beginning to live again.'

Ross nodded. 'Fine, but that's no excuse to go dashing back to work. Your body may be ready but your mind may not be. It's a common mistake. Before you know it you would be right back where you started.'

Janey squinted at Ross. 'You know, you sound more like my analyst every day. Are you sure you're not a doctor, or is this your writers' analytical mind working overtime?'

Ross laughed. 'I've been enjoying myself too. I can't ever remember enjoying myself so much. So I have ulterior motives for you not dashing off. Purely self-interest, I'm afraid.'

Janey affected awe and surprise. 'Well,' she said, slowly, savouring the moment. 'Is the ice beginning to crack?'

'I don't know what you mean,' responded Ross, stuffily. As he looked at Janey after this his gaze went out across her shoulder.

Without turning Janey asked: 'What is it?'

'Your steed arriveth.'

Janey turned around to see the pony standing a few feet behind her.

'It's very odd,' announced Janey. 'He always seems to find me - rather than the other way round.'

She walked up to him and stroked his nose.

Then she put on him the head-collar she had been carrying.

'Yes,' she decided, aloud. 'You've certainly been used before.' Then: 'You're so good I might enter you with Ross in a class.'

Ross and Janey laughed at the absurdity of such a vision. Then all three walked off, Ross and Janey nudging each other playfully.

It was a small show, just like hundreds of others taking place at weekends through the Summer and Autumn in England. Even now, at the end of Autumn, there was plenty of activity. Apart from games going on were a couple of fenced off 'rings' where show-jumping was in progress, watched by small groups of people and horse and rider pairs waiting their turn to compete.

Janey was by now one of this latter group, sat on the pony. The tack gleamed and the pony's coat shone. Janey was wearing proper riding dress and a bib that had '482' written on it. Beside her a girl was wearing Janey's coat and shoes.

As she sat there watching the competitor in the ring and looking out over the crowd she thought she recognised someone, a face. Then she saw the couple. It was Mr & Mrs Armitage and they were some way off in a small group near the entrance to the ring. Mrs Armitage waved and Janey responded.

Janey looked down to the girl. 'Very good of you to loan me your riding kit,' said Janey. 'Hope I stay on.'

The girl smiled.

Ross approached them from the ring. He was excited. 'Two have jumped all the fences and got none down.'

'Two clears,' responded Janey. 'Well at least there'll be a jump off. I can't think I'll be among them.'

'I won't, that's for sure,' offered the girl. 'I had the planks down. You've got to bring them back or they just flatten and take the top off.'

'Which is why they stick them at the end of a triple -jump so that you have to work really hard to slow down and bring the horse under you,' said Janey, surprising herself that long forgotten aspects of show-jumping were coming back to her.

Ross looked confused. 'That's easy for you to say,' he said. 'Whatever you said I'm sure you'll do well.'

'I think we're getting ahead of ourselves,' replied Janey, nervously. 'I've never jumped this one before - except for the practice jump just now.'

'You looked very comfortable,' said the girl. 'You've ridden before.' It was a statement, not a question.

Janey wasn't comfortable now though. 'But a very long time ago,' she said, by way of mitigation of what might come to pass. 'Being comfortable in the practice ring is a long way from being the same in the competition, as you know.'

'Too right,' confirmed the girl.

Mrs Armitage had come closer and was smiling. Mr Armitage appeared, carrying—with extravagant care—two brimming plastic cups.

'Come on. Let's not be defeatist,' said Ross, cheerfully, clapping his hands for effect. The pony reared. Fortunately, Janey stayed in the saddle. Behind them Mr Armitage stood with half-empty cups, wetness on his overcoat, and a look of disgust on his face.

'Well sat,' adjudged the girl.

'Sorry,' said Ross.

'I've just heard them call your number,' said the girl.

'Oh,' responded Janey, pulling a face.

'Good luck,' offered the girl. 'You'll be fine.'

The girl and Ross exchanged glances while Janey walked the pony away.

Janey spoke to the pony: 'So, little 'un. Not quite bomb proof, are we?'

Janey rode the pony into the ring. The fences were small, no more than a metre high. Slowly she walked the pony around and then the starting bell sounded.

Mrs Armitage was at the ringside near the first jump by now and was joined by her husband, carrying two more cups. Mrs Armitage encouraged him to hurry up and join her.

Janey quickened the pace to a trot, then to a canter and set up for the first jump. At the point of take-off the pony jinked and knocked the fence down.

Ross and the girl cringed and shook their heads.

Janey spoke to the pony in a low voice as she cantered to the next fence. 'My fault. Just a little rusty. Steady. You're doing fine.'

They took the next three jumps without difficulty.

Then she turned for triple-jump which she managed well and was not going too fast on the exit.

In front of her were the planks.

'Shorten up, Janey,' she whispered to herself. 'Power not speed.'

She approached the jump.

'That's it,' she announced, as she got to the point of take-off. The pony jumped the planks and tapped the top one. The plank swung in the cups.

Janey looked back very briefly and saw that the plank stayed up.

She jumped the rest of the jumps before the last with ease. The last was positioned so that the horse or pony would have to pass the exit before turning to do the last jump. It was an old ruse by course builders because the horse would naturally want to leave the ring. It was up to the rider to keep the horse or pony focused on the job in hand and not 'run out'.

As she passed the place where she had had the first fence down the pony jinked again but this time Janey was ready and rode the pony strongly to the last fence.

Even as the pony took off Janey knew she had cleared the last. She was already beaming.

She trotted out of the ring, patting the pony on its neck. Then she stopped and was joined by Ross and the girl.

'Shame about the first but the rest was good,' commiserated the girl.

'You knocked it down,' observed Ross. 'Are you disappointed.'

'Disappointed? No way! It was bloody brilliant. What a smashing horse.'

Janey dismounted with a flourish and moved to kiss the pony on the side of its face.

'Sunny would love this,' she gasped. 'She'd love you,' she said, kissing the horse. Then, reflectively, she said: 'Sunny.'

Ross was smiling. 'Thinking of your family. Definitely on the mend.' Then he turned away. His expression was briefly sad.

Janey and Ross were sat at the table corner as on the previous evening.

They were just finishing their drinks but it was noticeable that Janey was drinking water and Ross was being fairly abstemious with the wine.

The door opened and Mrs Armitage popped her head in and looked at Ross, inquiringly.

'Yes, fine, Mrs Armitage,' he said. 'I think we can manage from here. Good night.'

Mrs Armitage retreated and closed the door.

Janey sighed and then smiled. 'A wonderful day.'

Ross affected boredom. 'For the umpteenth time.'

'Well, it was. Thank you.'

'Don't thank me, Janey. You deserve it.'

'Still… ' Janey paused, then: 'You know, I'd forgotten you could have so much fun.'

'You may have thought you were in control when you were working in London. But it's more likely the job controlled you. Schedules to keep to. A routine that gave you no social life to speak of. You need to take control.'

Janey laughed.

'What?'

'Most people say I'm a control freak,' she said. Then she paused, thinking. 'You know, I agree with you. I've been the one controlled.'

The conversation lapsed for a couple of seconds into an awkward silence.

'I think I will have that drink after all,' said Janey, at last.

'Wine or something stronger.'

'Wine will be fine.'

Ross filled her glass with red wine. Then he poured himself a brandy.

Janey drank half of the glassful of wine in one gulp.

Ross raised an inquiring eyebrow.

'I haven't taken any pills today,' said Janey, by way of mitigation. 'I didn't feel I needed to.'

'Is that a good idea?'

Ross waited but Janey didn't answer. Ross swirled his brandy around the glass. 'Well, you know best,' he said, resignedly.

'I didn't thank you for not taking advantage of me last night.' Janey looked down at her glass, preferring not to meet his gaze.

'I prefer to practice my seduction technique on the fairly sober, and,' he paused, smiling, 'for more practical purposes, it helps if I am too.'

Janey smiled. 'Over the past few days we've talked about most subjects under the sun. What do you know about seduction?'

Ross was on the point of taking a sip from his drink but managed to spill it instead. 'Er. Oh, the usual. I find it best not to rush things.'

'I'm beginning to realise that,' said Janey quietly, looking into his eyes.

'I'll ignore that,' he said. He put a hand over hers. She didn't move it.

'When I have finished with the preliminaries I move on to the practical,' explained Ross.

Ross moved his chair nearer. 'May I ...kiss you?'

'Hmm,' murmured Janey, her tone non-committal.

'Perhaps you can help?' suggested Ross.

Janey shook her head slowly. 'No. You take the lead. It's your seduction technique we're demonstrating, er, discussing.'

'It's going wrong already,' said Ross, disappointed. 'You're not responding.'

Janey moved closer and in a tone that was sleepy, said: 'Oh. How do you want me to respond?'

'Well, I kiss you like this,' he said, and kissed her. 'Then like this.' Another kiss. 'And then...'

Janey, enjoying this: 'You're sure this isn't a work of fiction still, a figment of your imagination?'

'More autobiographical, actually.'

Janey was impatient, but not hurried. 'At the rate you're going you'll be ninety before I learn your seduction technique. Perhaps we should cut a few corners.' She rose and took his hand in hers. 'Follow me.'

'What are you doing?' said Ross, intrigued but following all the same.

'Doing as you suggested,' she said. 'I'm taking control.'

'Yes, Miss. All very well, of course, but you seem to have moved from my seduction technique to one of my fantasies.'

'And you're complaining?'

'No.'

'Then, shhh. You're too intellectual by half.'

Janey guided him to the door.

Chapter Twelve

Ross was sat at the breakfast table reading a book.

Mrs Armitage put the toast-rack on the table as Janey entered the room and took her place silently.

'What would you like, madam? We have …'

Janey avoided eye contact. 'Just a piece of toast and some coffee, please.'

Ross smiled. 'Good morning.'

Janey finally looked up, her expression frail, pleading for understanding.

Ross looked again at his book again and frowned.

'I came across this book in the library. Thought you'd be interested.'

'Oh?'

Ross persevered. 'It was written by a local. Local history. Private publisher, that sort of thing. There's a bit about a previous tenant of the cottage you tried to destroy.'

Janey smiled, weakly.

'She painted the painting you told me about. Someone called 'E. Stewart.''

'Breaking Waves?' Janey was suddenly interested.

'Seems she spent a summer painting it. When she disappeared…'

'Disappeared?'

'That's what it says here. Anyway, she wasn't just a bad painter; she was a pretty bad poet as well. Seems she was trying to do what you're doing, breaking the cycle. Except she called it breaking waves.'

Ross picked up the book and turned a page. 'Listen to this.

"Breaking waves.
 The rolling seas run rough or light,
 Echoing life's ups and downs.
The crests and troughs lift and fall,
 And in both good and bad are found.
Nature's way joins both in turn,
 Building and sundering per plan.
Some would see their lives the same,
 A sequence they can understand.
And in this way you stay the same,
 As most who stride this Earth.
Who take their lot as all they've got,
 As Nature's way unchanged.
But there are those, who shirk such plans,
 And rail against Nature's way.
They change the way their lives do run,
 We call it breaking waves."'

'I have to agree with you,' said Janey. 'Disappeared.'

'Don't think she was the full article. Still struggling to find out what she wanted. The painting, poem and other writings were left in the cottage. No other trace of her. Tragic.'

Janey frowned. 'What, that she disappeared, or that she didn't find what she was looking for.'

'Quite. She probably just upped sticks and ran out of sheer frustration at not being able to express herself.'

'What's the other book', queried Janey, nodding at a small, well used paperback on the table.

Ross picked it up. 'Interesting little tome,' he said, flicking the pages. 'Time-lining, it says.'

'What?'

Ross handed the book to her. 'I had a look through earlier. It must be something she used to help her.'

'It's a self-help book,' decided Janey, throwing it back on the table.

Ross frowned. 'It's a simple procedure anyone can do, I understand.'

'To do what?' Janey was uninterested.

'Well, as far as I can make out you use it to go back through your history and rediscover things and events which you may have forgotten or your brain has shut out.'

'A sort of memory jogger.'

'A bit more than that, it seems,' he said, quickly. 'What you're trying to do is remember the bad things in life and lay the ghosts to rest. It's about banishing bad memories which may have changed your life. No, damaged your life.'

'You seem to know a lot about it,' said Janey, suspicious.

'Only what I read earlier. The idea is that you lay these ghosts to rest and that means you will rid yourself of pressure points that are impacting your life now. They give an example: say you were in a car crash as a little girl.'

Janey sat up. 'You knew that,' she accused him.

It was Ross's turn to be angry. He picked up the book and found a particular page. He showed it to Janey. 'There. That's the example they used. Not everything is about you, Janey.'

Janey recoiled.

Ross realised he'd gone too far. 'Sorry,' he said, quickly.

They were quiet for a few moments. It was Janey who broke the silence. 'What about the example?'

'It doesn't matter,' said Ross, dismissively. 'It's probably all gobbled-gook, anyway.'

'No, go on,' she encouraged.

Ross sighed. 'Well, the idea is that if you had a bad memory like that and it had left you with a fear which was affecting your life because it happened when you were a child and couldn't deal with it, then when you time-lined back, revisited it, you would re-live it in your mind but with the maturity you had now rather than as a child. Also, because it wasn't actually happening, just a memory, remembering it wouldn't be so painful and your brain would put it into the 'no big deal' box, where it belonged. The problems you had been experiencing as a result of the experience might then disappear.'

'American book, is it? she asked, but there was a faint hint of interest in her voice.

'Yes, as it happens,' said Ross, looking at the cover of the book. 'Why do you ask?'

'The 'no big deal' was a give-away.' She smiled. 'I wonder if it works? No, I wonder how it works.'

'Do you want to try it? I think I've picked up the gist of it.'

Janey pretended to be nervous. 'Oooh, we'll make a trick-cyclist out of you yet,' she said.

Ross ignored this. 'Well, okay. You lie back…'

'…and think of England?' she interrupted. 'This sounds interesting.'

'Be serious,' he said. 'Lie back and close your eyes.'

'Yes, sir,' she answered, but got herself comfortable in a reclining position on the settee and closed her eyes.

'Right. The idea is to go back in time by starting off with this morning, then yesterday and keep going. It doesn't matter if you can't remember everything just keep going back a month, a year, five years remembering the good but allowing time for you to remember the bad.'

'That'll take ages,' she protested.

'You're right,' he admitted. 'Try going back *from* when you were say, ten or so.'

'Ten. Right,' she said. 'Agoo. Gurgle, gurgle.'

'This is silly,' he said, frustrated by her antics.

'Oh. Ten years not ten months,' she said, hurriedly. 'I've got it.'

After a three minutes of silence he said: 'Where are you now.'

'At the Grange,' she answered.

Ross sighed. 'Well, if you're not going to take this seriously…..'

'No,' she interrupted, still with her eyes shut. 'I'll behave. I'm back at school, eleven years old. I remember … I'm in the car with Eric…. Huh!'

'What is it?' Ross moved to her side.

'No, don't Ross,' she pleaded. 'Let me finish this. I only want to do it once.'

Ross moved back, tense.

Janey's love for organisation had started when she first began to study her mother. 'There had to be a better way,' she had told herself. Even at the age of eleven-years-old she had known her mother was scatter-brained and decided never to be so disorganised.

Her mother had been driving the car in which Eric, Janey's boyfriend of the time, was travelling with her on the school run at the end of the day. As usual, mother had a hundred things on her mind. Mother wasn't a good driver and Janey preferred to sit in the back seat when it was her mother's turn to do the trip. Eric had no such qualms and preferred to sit in the front passenger seat— 'shotgun', as he called it— even if it meant he wouldn't be close to Janey. Of course, had Janey wanted him to be in the back seat with her he would have jolly well done as he was told. She was already developing her strong character.

This particular trip Eric had been looking back to Janey, talking as they drove down the winding country lane. This position was difficult to maintain with the seatbelt on so he had taken if off.

Her mother was also talking, her attention split so that only occasionally was her attention fleetingly directed to her driving and the tractor which was ahead of her. Janey's mother wasn't good in stressful situations and the crocodile of traffic behind their car seemed to pressure her to overtake. Several times she moved out only to have to pull back abruptly when oncoming traffic appeared. Still, she had continued to try while Eric continued his conversation with Janey.

Then it happened. They were on the straight bit, with a clear road ahead. Her mother abruptly pulled out and accelerated. Unfortunately, a side turning in front of the tractor hid a car which pulled out to turn right, right into their car. It had all happened so suddenly. Eric disappeared through the windscreen and the front of the car came back to trap her mother's legs. Janey was in shock and froze.

First on the scene were other car drivers, one of whom led Janey away from the gruesome sight and along the road the way they had been travelling. As he did so they heard the ambulance or fire-engine arriving and her helper turned to see them arrive. While he did so Janey continued, seeing a brown paper bag ahead of her. As she drew closer she had the intention of picking it up as it was untidy. Then, from several feet away from the object she saw it for what it was: the brown was the brown of Eric's hair and the object was his head.

It would be several days before she was able to talk without bursting into tears.

Throughout the days of visits to her mother in hospital, the whiplash she herself had suffered, Eric's funeral, she was like an automaton. Gradually thereafter she began to appear normal and to return to some kind of order but she never addressed the car crash and Eric's loss in any way that was obvious to others. Some thought she had mentally blotted out the accident. Time passed until it was just another patched problem, another 'kink in the spine', to be ignored as one worked out one's life.

'Janey,' it was Ross, a note of concern in his voice.

Janey began to cry. 'Poor Eric. He never had a chance.'

Ross put his arms around her. 'I'm sorry,' he soothed. 'I shouldn't have done this. It was a stupid idea.'

Janey opened her eyes but was silent for a few moments. Then she said: 'I'm not sure I believe this will work but I've been avoiding revisiting that scene for years. I'm not sure I even remembered.'

'It does say in the book that your mind can shut things off because of the pain, a self-defence mechanism or something.'

Janey was calm, almost spaced out. 'Well, I'm not sure I believe it – perhaps you have to do it a few times - but… Thank you, Ross.' Her gaze was serious and her gratitude was clear for him to see.

'It was nothing,' he blustered.

'It was,' she disagreed. 'Thank you for caring.'

Ross looked away and was distracted at that moment by something he saw outside and turned his head to get a better view. Then he stood up, relieved at the interruption.

'Your friend is here,' he announced, pointing out of the window to the lawn where the pony was grazing. 'I don't think Mr Armitage is too happy. He spent enough time yesterday filling in the divets.'

'I must go out to him,' said Janey, rising.

Ross put a restraining hand on her arm. 'He'll keep. He's quite happy winding up Mr Armitage for the moment.' His expression became concerned. 'Are you all right?' He paused. 'About last night?'

Janey's shoulders sagged. 'Yes,' she sighed. 'It was beautiful. Unfortunately, quite beautiful.

'Heap good medicine, but regrets. Yes?' suggested Ross.

Janey smiled, weakly. 'Yes.'

Mrs Armitage was looking from the kitchen window onto the lawn where Janey and Ross were gentling the pony. Mr Armitage was sat at the kitchen table reading a newspaper.

Mrs Armitage shook her head. 'It's not the same. Something's changed with those two.'

Mr Armitage was distracted. 'Not as far as I'm concerned. You'd think I'd nothing else to do but clear up after that animal. It shouldn't be on the lawn. Gawd knows what the boss'll have to say.'

Mrs Armitage might not have heard him, she is talking to herself. 'The strain is still in her, but...,' she paused, 'it's a different strain. You don't think they got too cosy last night, d'you? I'd've given up a week's soaps to have been witness to that.'

Janey was talking to the pony. 'We missed you.'

'He doesn't say much, does he,' observed Ross, feeling a little left out of this relationship.

'Very funny. Horses pick up more than most people think. Like dogs they pick up on moods. They're very sensitive to our emotions, which is why we should always be calm in their company.'

The pony moved away and walked from the lawn into the distance.

'Well, he seems to have picked up on the mood here,' said Ross.

Ross and Janey were sat in the lounge. The tea things were still on the small table. Her painting was propped up on the mantle-piece. There was tension in the air.

Outside the snow was falling and beginning to settle, driven by a strong breeze.

'What do you want to do?' Ross's tone was gentle.

Janey got up abruptly and studied the painting, her back to Ross. The almost finished canvas was not the success she had seen in her mind's eye all those weeks ago. The scene could be made out but the brush strokes were uneven and amateur. Still, so long as the viewer was some distance from the painting a reasonable assumption could be discerned as to the scene it was trying to depict.

144

'There's obviously more to this painting than I'd imagined,' she announced.

'I think it's wonderful. I love it,' he said.

'You're kidding,' said Janey, genuinely surprised.

'No, I mean it. I really, really like it.'

Janey turned back to face him. There were tears in her eyes.

'What do you want to do?' Ross's tone was more insistent.

'What do you mean?'

'You know what I mean, Janey,' explained Ross. 'We've broken the vows. You've been looking radiant. You may find it difficult to go back to Luke after...'

'Don't call him Luke, you don't know him. He's my husband,' she said quickly. Then: 'And I don't know what to do. If you want, I'll move back to the cottage. I've still a bit more work on the painting to do. Then I'll go home.'

'Back to the fray,' decided Ross. 'And me? I'll just carry on with my, er, research as if nothing has happened, shall I. Sad, but not bitter.'

'Yes,' said Janey sympathetically. 'We've - I've - had a wonderful time and you are a wonderful man. Going any further would surely spoil it...'

'... but you have to go,' confirmed Ross.

'I don't want to go,' she said, quietly.

Ross went over to Janey and they kissed, their passion rising again.

In the psychiatrist's office, David was dressed in casual clothes. In front of him, on the desk, was an open folder. He was holding a phone to his ear while his eyes scanned the document. He was reading it for the third time.

At the other end of the phone Luke was a little distracted, watching Sunny playing on the floor.

David was speaking: 'I've just read the results from Janey's blood test. Sorry it's taken so long. I only just got back from holiday.'

'Huh-huh,' responded Luke.

'There are traces of Benzedrine,' began David. 'What you might know as uppers. I'll correct that - large amounts of uppers. She must have been fit to scream even without the stress from her work. D'you know anything about this?'

It was fortunate that David couldn't see Luke's face. He also couldn't know that Luke was putting a lot of effort into projecting a tone that was matter-of-fact when he spoke. 'You know Janey,' he answered. 'Her own worst enemy at times. Could be she was taking them to get through the day. As you know, she wasn't sleeping much at night.'

'Didn't you see them, Luke? These are large doses.'

'Do you think I'd have let her take them if I'd known?' Luke's tone was defensive.

'As you say, Janey has a mind of her own. She's not taking them now, is she?'

'I did her packing for the trip. She definitely didn't take any from here.'

'Well, that's something. How's she getting on?'

'Fine,' said Luke. 'She's getting along fine.'

The bed was dishevelled and Janey's form was alone under the covers. There was the sound of a man's voice, indistinct, but outside the bedroom. It was a telephone call.

Janey moved restlessly as the noise woke her. Then a window flew open ballooning the curtains and bringing in a shower of snowflakes. Almost instantly she got out of bed and shut the window before restoring the curtains. Then she got back into bed.

She closed her eyes and tried to return to sleep but the activity of shutting the window had brought her to full wakefulness and there was no way back. Now she heard someone talking and she opened her eyes again, her head craned to one side as she tried to make out what was being said.

Ross was using the telephone in the hallway, attired in his dressing gown. As he talked, he was absent-mindedly sifting through the photos in the biscuit tin, which was open on the hall table.

'I don't care,' he said. 'I'm calling it off now.' He paused. 'No.' He winced. 'Nothing has happened. I just don't want to go on with this any longer.'

Ross turned his head in response to a noise on the landing above and he saw Janey. Then his tone changed. 'Publish and be damned!' he said into the instrument and slammed down the phone.

Janey, clutching a dressing gown around her said: 'Is everything all right?'

'Bloody publishers,' said Ross. Then he moved up the stairs and they returned to the bedroom.

'I'm going to take a bath,' he announced. Then he went into the bathroom and closed the door.

Slightly affronted by his brusqueness and unconvinced by what he had said in his telephone call, Janey moved back to the landing and down to the hall. Then she picked up the phone and pressed the redial button.

She wrote the answer on the pad. It was the same as that which Gerry had dialled. The last four numbers were: 7474.

Janey was shocked: it was her home number.

'Hello?' said Luke. 'Hello?'

Janey, shocked at hearing Luke's voice put down the phone, but incorrectly. It didn't sit on the cradle properly. On impulse she picked up the biscuit tin.

Minutes later Ross came out of the bathroom. He looked around, noticing that Janey wasn't there. Then he noticed that her clothes were missing from the chair where they had lain.

'Janey?' called Ross, softly.

When there was no reply he moved along the corridor to Janey's room.

At her door, Ross knocked lightly. 'Janey?'

Ross tried the door and it opened. He looked inside and the bedroom was neat and tidy with no sign of habitation. He looked at the packages she had bought with her to the Grange. The backpack was missing and so were her parka and other weather clothes. He looked at the window and saw the swirling snow outside and heard the frame of the window rattle from the force of the wind.

'My God!' he cried, frightened. 'She's gone out … and in this weather.'

Ross looked briefly towards the window again before turning about and running towards his bedroom.

Luke tried to call the Grange but the telephone was busy. He replaced the phone.

Then he began pacing up and down.

The door opened slowly. Sunny appeared, rubbing her eyes. She'd been crying.

'Daddy. I'm frightened,' she cried.

Luke lifted her to him.

'It was just a bad dream again, darling. No more bad dreams.'

The phone rang.

Chapter Thirteen

Janey was wearing her backpack and carrying the biscuit tin under her arm. She wasn't sure how long she had been trudging through the snow, through the blackness of the night, but she knew that the biscuit tin under her arm was uncomfortable and a distraction. It was bad enough that she was having great difficulty moving through this weather at all. So she stopped and put the tin in her backpack, itself a protracted operation as she had to take off her backpack, unfasten the binding and place the tin inside before re-securing the backpack, all the while coping with the swirling snow.

Becoming increasingly worried about her predicament, miles from anywhere, she had only one response - keep moving - and so she did not delay after donning the backpack once more.

As she walked, the wind and snow whipping at her face and body, stumbling through the uneven ground coated by an ever thicker carpet of snow and through flurries of the white stuff that appeared to be falling almost horizontally, she recounted the evidence, the realisations that had prompted her flight from the Grange.

She remembered Ross's behaviour, his asking her to join him at the Grange. She remembered his response when she told him of the face at the window. Hardly shocked, she had thought at the time. That was because it was him, she now decided. Then there was his decision—against her wishes — not to involve the police over the photographs. She was even suspicious of his falling out with George and his knowledge of the woman who painted Breaking Waves. What was worse was that she had trusted him completely and now she felt betrayed.

Then her frantic mind turned to Luke, recounting his observation that they'd not been close and, she remembered bitterly, his words: 'I'll organise it. I'll bloody organise it, alright!'.

'Why, Luke? Why?' shouted Janey, into the wind. Then: 'Divorce?' The word shocked her and she realised this was his aim - had been his aim all along. 'Sunny!' she cried. 'He wants to take Sunny away from me!'

The snow was already deep and she slipped and slid as she tried to find her way to the cottage through the blizzard that was growing ever stronger. She was becoming very frightened and on the point of being lost when she saw a hedge which, even covered in snow, she thought might just be one of the landmarks only a hundred-or-so yards from the cottage.

Every so often she peered into the darkness behind her, imagining that someone was following her.

At the Grange, Ross was holding the phone. He was very agitated.

'Luke! She's gone,' he said. Then: 'The cottage. Where else?'

He heard a door open and realised he'd been shouting. He looked to the window. When he spoke he struggled to keep his voice low. 'It's snowing here, too. I'm going after her.'

At the other end of the line, Luke replaced the phone. He was still holding Sunny with one arm.

His expression was frightened. 'What have I done?'

He looked through the window, where it was snowing steadily. Then he picked up the phone and dialled a number.

'Hello,' he began. 'I used your helicopter services recently. Yes. Luke Holland. I need your help - and fast. It's an emergency.' He paused. 'Tonight. Oh. When's it expected to clear.' He looked at Sunny, sleeping against his shoulder. 'No, I understand. I.....we'll be there even before dawn. Yes. We'll be waiting for you.'

Janey almost stumbled upon the cottage, it's black shape just visible against the snow. On the way she had come round to the idea that she would seek sanctuary with George and Margaret but the weather had dissuaded her from trudging the extra mile. She now decided she would call them and, after she'd got her breath back, make the trip to their house.

Once inside the cottage, and with this new plan in mind, she moved in the darkness to where she thought she had left the mobile phone. It wasn't there. Feeling around in the dark she couldn't find it but she blundered across the torch and switched it on.

Then she looked around for the phone. She found it on the breakfast table and hurriedly picked up both halves. As she did so she saw moisture on the table where they had lain.

Janey screamed with anguish. 'Oh, no! Please don't tell me I still can't use the phone.' Then: 'Gotta dry it out.'

She rubbed the outer casing of each half of the phone on her jeans. Then she shook her head.

'No, no. Think,' she told herself. 'The damp is inside.'

She lit the hurricane lamp. Then she placed the halves of the mobile upright against the sides of the lamp. 'It might work,' she said, then corrected herself: 'It has to work.'

Ross was standing at the same spot where Janey had stowed away the biscuit tin into her backpack. He'd paused there because he could just discern the uneven snow where Janey had stopped briefly and placed the backpack on the snow. He peered ahead. The blizzard was worsening but fortunately he had a torch and could see that the foot marks were large and well defined in the snow ahead. They headed straight for the cottage.

Ross covered his eyes against the snow as he looked about him. 'Janey!' he called. 'Janey!' Then he listened for a second before dropping his head into the oncoming snow flurries and trudged on.

Inside the cottage Janey looked to the door and saw the flimsy, damaged, lock. Then she looked around briefly before she moved over to the closet and struggled to move it against the door. As she did this, she caught the table bearing the biscuit tin and the wad of documents and photographs fell out.

Grappling with the closet, Janey only had time to register that the biscuit tin had spilled onto the floor. Hurriedly, she finished off the barricading.

Now that she had nothing to do but wait she was feeling very scared.

As she sat there, wondering what to do next, she glanced again at the biscuit tin and reached over to retrieve it and its contents from the floor.

She hadn't looked too closely at the photos before but now she sifted through all the contents of the box.

Slowly she picked up each piece and studied it. There was the child's poem; pressed flowers on a piece of cardboard; photos of a girl in summer wear on a beach; some less savoury photographs, and; some with a man in them, but Janey couldn't quite see his face.

Then she picked up the last piece.

The last document wasn't a photo, it was a folded sketch. It was the sketch Janey had made for the picture, together with the doodle of the pony, and Ross.

At this discovery Janey gasped, suddenly feeling very vulnerable. She looked around as if sensing danger, and glanced at the window. She saw a man's face there.

Janey screamed. The face had already disappeared. She hurried over to the window and pulled the curtains across it.

'I am not imagining these things,' she shouted, angrily. But her courage was waning. 'How am I going to get out of here?' she said to herself, crying. 'I can't go now... I'll have to hold out till morning then somehow ...'

Then Janey saw a light through the curtains at the window.

She had turned around to stare at the window when she heard a loud bang at the door. She screamed again.

'It's Ross. Janey, let me in.'

'Stay away from me,' she shouted back, terrified. 'I -I've got a knife.'

Janey scurried over to the kitchen area and rummaged among the cutlery, and quickly selected a large mean-looking bread knife.

'It's hell out here, Janey,' he called. 'Let me in. We have to talk. What have I done? Have I upset you? What made you make this mad journey?'

'You can't come in,' she replied. 'I saw you through the window. You've been calling my home. What are you and Luke planning?'

'Janey. Janey,' he pleaded. 'You've got it all wrong. Let me in. I'm freezing out here.' Then: 'All right. I admit I looked through the window the first night you were here. I just wanted to know you were safe. Now let me in.'

'That's a lie! You've been looking through most nights. You were looking through the window just now.'

Janey. I promise I wasn't. Why would I lie? I've only just got here.'

Janey was puzzled. 'Then who was it?' she said to herself, shaking.

Outside, Ross was crouched by the door. 'Janey!' he pleaded, his voice raised against the noise of the blizzard. Then he abruptly looked around him but could n't see anything that had prompted the feeling that he was not alone.

Had he been able to turn around a little farther he would have seen the figure of a man who was wielding a knife and coming straight towards him.

Janey stared at the door.

'I'm sorry,' said Ross. 'Luke asked me to keep an eye on you. He really loves you. It seemed a good idea but things went a bit too far. I was trying to tell him I couldn't go on with looking after you. I didn't say why, of course, but I felt we were getting too serious. That we were going to cause more problems than we solved. Janey. Janey, please let me in...' Then he screamed.

Janey could hear the sound of a struggle against the door, followed by another scream.

'Ross?'

Janey pulled the barricade back a little and opened the door.

Ross was lying on the ground. There was no sign of anyone else. Janey opened the door and dragged him in.

'Close the door,' gasped Ross. 'He's still close by. I gave him some of his own medicine with his knife.' With that he lifted his right hand and revealed a deep cut across his palm. 'Took some effort getting it off him, mind you. He's badly injured but, unfortunately, I'm afraid..,' he added, his face pale, '..so am I.'

Janey managed to get him to the armchair. Then she pulled away his left hand, which he had been using to support his side. It was covered in blood.

She grabbed a shirt and pushed it in the place where the blood was seeping through his shirt and replaced his hand.

'Bit late to become practical,' he panted. 'But I'm not complaining. You'd better push that thing..,' he said, glancing at the closet, '..against the door.

'Who is it? What does he want?' Janey's voice was tremulous.

'I can't be sure,' said Ross, having difficulty speaking. 'I couldn't make him out in the dark, but I think it's our friend George Smith.'

'What, the man at the cottage? George?'

Ross tried to nod. 'The only man I know who still wears one of these.' He held up the deerstalker that was in his other hand. 'He should be getting quite cold out there.'

'Did you bring your mobile?'

'Fraid not, Janey. You didn't give me time.'

'Oh, God. Mine's still waterlogged,' she complained.

Janey looked over to the hurricane lamp and Ross followed her gaze. There was a slight whiff of smoke coming from one half of the phone.

'I'm trying to dry it out,' she explained.

'Better move it away from there, or it'll only be good for making smoke signals.'

The figure of a man was sitting on the ground, his back to the blizzard. He had a scarf wrapped around his head, which covered most of his face. The coat collar was up around his neck. He was gasping and groaning, in obvious pain. Then he felt inside his long coat and brought out a torch. He shone the torch at the ground about him and saw the knife, covered in blood, and reached out a hand to retrieve it.

Then he struggled to his feet and staggered off. After a few steps he wavered and dropped to a knee. Then, with a grunt, he struggled again to his feet and moved on.

Janey put the two halves of the mobile phone on the breakfast table. Then she turned quickly and looked at the door. She nodded. 'He fixed the lock,' she announced. 'That's how he got in. And I found a sketch of mine in the box. It went missing when I was here last. It was buried at the bottom.'

'I thought you must have taken the box,' said Ross, his breathing more laboured. 'I hate to say it but he's probably building up the same sick dossier on you that he did for that poor girl.' Then: 'Does he know you've found it?'

'I think he was at the window when I was looking through the box just now.'

'That explains the attack,' said Ross. 'I knew there was bad blood between us but I feel he's taken this a tad too far, don't you? Something in the box must tie him to his daughter's death. I don't want to frighten you but I think he wants it back and he's proved he's prepared to kill us if necessary.'

They heard a sound and both Janey and Ross looked at the door.

The bar of the lock retracted and the door handle turned.

'Turn out the light,' ordered Ross, in a croaked whisper.'

Before she could get away Ross grabbed her arm. He was near to losing consciousness.

'Janey, you've got..to..get..help. I'll try to hold him up. Just get clear. Either direction along the cliff. Should..,' he was struggling to speak, '.. find a house. Ross reached for the torch and held it on his chest.

'I'll do my best,' said Janey, gravely.

Chapter Fourteen

The door opened and a hand holding a knife appeared.

Then the hurricane lamp flickered and dimmed. In the moment before the illumination faded to nothing it was possible to make out the shapes of the three people in the cottage.

As the man stumbled over the barricade trying to get to Janey he was landed a heavy blow on the head by Ross's raised but extinguished torch.

The torch switched on from the jolt and parts of the figure were illuminated dimly. Janey, meanwhile, was trying to get over the rubble of the barricade to the open door. The man was groggy and stumbled over the wreckage and attacked Ross, raining blows on him and beating him senseless.

Although in a rage the figure still detected Janey as she moved to the door and he leapt to intercept her. Janey had, meanwhile, found the knife she had been holding before and now plunged it through the man's thick coat. He screamed and moved for the door. Rebounding off the jamb he fell out into the snow once more.

Almost at the same instance, Janey was also out of the cottage and moving as best she could in the blizzard towards the cliff.

She hadn't progress very far before she fell in the darkness. Even so, she recognised the spot by the slight elevation of the ground. It was the same place she had fallen off the pony. It was only yards from the edge of the cliff.

Carefully, she tried to retrace her steps, walking backwards. 'Where's the edge?' Her voice was distraught. 'I can't see the edge!'

Then a bloody hand settled on her shoulder. She turned, shocked, but could not see the face of her attacker.

Janey screamed.

They struggled and she lashed out blindly. Even though he landed several blows he was as hampered by the darkness and blizzard as she was and his blows lacked any focus. Finally, she managed to throw her weight into him and he collapsed to the ground.

Desperate to get away from her attacker she headed wildly into the blizzard and soon had no idea where she was or in which direction she was heading.

When Ross came round he shone the torch at the breakfast table and illuminated the mobile phone bits. Then he struggled to the breakfast table and managed to retrieve the two halves of the phone and the battery.

As he slumped back onto the sofa he kicked the small table bearing the biscuit tin. His eyes turned to look at the source of the noise and he saw a particular photograph. The background was of a horse show and the girl, Rosie, was sat on the pony. In the background was a suspicious looking character, wearing a deerstalker hat. He peered at the photograph, feeling he recognised the face. Then it hit him. 'Armitage,' he exclaimed.

For a moment or so he was in shock. Then he recovered a little. 'It isn't George. It's Armitage. But why?' Then: 'The photograph. He's been trying to recover this photograph. Janey!'

With difficulty he checked for alignment of the battery with the mobile phone proper. On the inside of the cover was a label bearing the number: *8888.*

Ross then put the two halves together and switched on the phone. The phone beeped and the screen came alive. It read: 'Enter pin number'.

Ross swore and looked confused.

Then he looked around and saw Janey's bag. With some effort he picked it up and emptied the contents on the floor.

There were myriad amounts of paper in there and Ross was overwhelmed with the task in front of him. He was close to unconsciousness now through loss of blood.

'I haven't got time,' he decided. 'I need a shortcut. Time to try to get into the female mind. Think man!'

Ross shuddered with the pain as he tried to remain conscious. Still, he forced himself to relax by resting his head and closing his eyes for a moment.

Suddenly, he opened them again and picked up the mobile phone. He switched it off and dismantled it. Then he looked at the label on the back of the phone: *8888*. He put the two halves back together and entered this number in response to the pin number query. The phone beeped.

He dialled 999 then collapsed back on the divan.

'Emergency service. Which service do you require?' said a voice.

Ross didn't respond. He was unconscious.

Janey stumbled on, lost and weakening from the efforts and shocks of the night.

Then she stopped and looked back the way she'd come. She tried hard to see through the blizzard but her eyes were narrowed to almost shut to avoid the snow. She was looking around, scared.

'Where am I?' She was crying. 'The Grange. I've got to get to the Grange. I've got to get help. Mr Armitage.'

Blindly she trudged on.

She looked over her shoulder again. She could see her small footprints, blurring fast but still visible. They were not straight but turned right in an arc as she had staggered on.

In front of her feet, other tracks appeared of the same size. Janey fell to her knees. She was almost covered in snow. 'Oh, no. I'm going round in circles.'

She bent her head to the ground, defeated. She was whimpering and soon began rocking backwards and forwards as the snow began to cover her.

Within minutes Janey had stopped moving two and fro and now she was shivering. Her mind began to wander and the kaleidoscope of events of the past few weeks ran before her eyes. One memory was of the time-lining and she lapsed once again into memories of her recent past. This one was from a year earlier; she was being congratulated on her promotion. Then she remembered being tasked to run a meeting, which would not have been a problem for her ordinarily. But these were not her usual colleagues, these were executives with no allegiance to her. Her audience were a different set of animals completely. At first she had been shocked but had left the meeting three hours later sweating and shaking from the grilling and abuse she had received. She had been completely unprepared for working with those who made simple if brutal decisions at the upper levels of the company. This wasn't management, this was street fighting, and gambling with very high stakes in international wheeler-dealing. This wasn't procedural, this was war and she hadn't known the rules and was left like a shell-shocked soldier from the trenches.

Gerry had 'debriefed' her, she remembered, but she had been in a trance. He hadn't the time to hand-hold her through the escalating pressure she felt and she had no clue how to combat the problems facing

her except to try to apply her old, low-level, management procedures which were wholly unsuited to the
battleground she had so recently entered.

This was it, she realised, sobbing as she knelt there
in the snow, alone, very cold and very afraid. This
was the final event which had led her to this point.
So simple, she decided. Her inflexibility had finally
hit a level of management where pragmatism was
everything; had to be. For her it had been a step, a
challenge, a brick wall too far.

Kneeling in the snow, she was fast disappearing
from view as it swirled about her. Soon she would be
completely covered, hardly discernable from the
mainly flat expanse of grey-white around her.

She wanted to give up now: just go to sleep and let
life go. She was at her lowest point. Broken at last,
despair her overriding emotion.

But something inside her just would not let her
give in. Like a last fluttering flame in a gutting fire,
the inflexibility that had driven her to breakdown
against—for her—an impossible situation at work,
prevented her from letting go completely. The flame
was a mixture of indignation and pure bloody stub-
bornness. She became angry and slightly crazy as she
railed against her situation. But now her emotion
wasn't purely self-centred as it had been for so long
in the past. Her epiphany of moments earlier had
turned her thoughts on their head. She was now
thinking of her family.

'Luke!' she cried out, this time in a plea for help.
'Sunny!' she cried, filling that one word with all the

guilt she had bottled up for putting her, she now saw, stupid, unimportant, job first.

Then, fearing that George would hear her she looked briefly around her, blinking the snow away from her eyes and breaking large lumps of snow from her body, as she moved, before looking straight ahead into the snow-swirling gloom.

Abruptly, she tensed as she saw a dark shape coming straight towards her.

'Oh, God. No. Not George!'

Janey searched about her wildly for somewhere to hide. She didn't know if there was anywhere to hide because she couldn't see anything more than a few feet in any direction and there was nothing to hide behind within that range. Then she looked back and peered closely at the emerging figure ready for whatever was her fate.

It was the pony, half covered in snow, walking towards her.

The pony approached, dropping his head to hers, and breathed hot air onto Janey's face. Then he moved to one side to halt next to Janey in the position she would be for mounting its back.

Janey was very weak and dazed by now and at first made no attempt to move. The pony moved its head round to nudge her, with sufficient force to push her to the ground. Sobbing, she got to her feet and reached for the pony's mane, trying with numbed fingers to get a good grip.

It was only the knowledge that if she didn't climb onto the pony she would die were she stood that made her able to attempt mounting in these conditions and without stirrups. It wasn't pretty but she succeeded in lying across the ponies back before managing an agonising change to a sitting position. All the time the pony stayed rock still. It was a minute or perhaps two before she had regained some sort of composure and her breath.

Holding on to the mane, she tried to push the pony in the direction she thought was the right one for the Grange but the pony resisted. She tried again; still he refused to move.

Janey couldn't understand this resistance so peered ahead. Suddenly she saw the problem; the cliff edge was only a few feet ahead of them and in the direction Janey had been walking. She also realised that it was only because she had gone around in circles earlier that she had avoided going over the cliff before.

Then, uncommanded, the pony turned and started walking along the cliff edge, with the cliff to its right.

Minutes later Janey was slumped, covered in snow, across the pony's back. The pony was still walking along the cliff but unsteadily.

The blizzard was very heavy now and the pony too was spooked. Janey, for her part tried to soothe the pony by talking about their experiences together from the first day of her arrival at the cottage to the show-jumping. But eventually she grew quiet as her exhaustion took over.

She knew she was fading away but couldn't quite give up. All the same, she knew she couldn't last much longer before she fell off into the deep snow from exhaustion. She also knew that the pony couldn't last much longer. The snow was thick and it was very difficult for the pony to negotiate. Still, Janey reflected, they would be together at the end.

Then a very bright light from directly ahead illuminated the pair, startling the pony.

He slipped and fell, tossing Janey into the deep snow. Then the light went out and the pony disappeared over the cliff.

When Janey recovered she could not see the pony and detected that the cliff edge was quite close.

For a few moments she felt sick. This is the end, she thought.

She wiped the snow from her face and peered around. Then she saw a light. It was dim but a light. She managed to get to her feet and moved closer.

One step followed another and soon the light was a little brighter and she could make out a building, which she quickly realised was very close. Spurred on by hope she staggered on, realising for the first time that she had injured her right leg in the fall and was now having to drag it along with great difficulty.

Sweating and doped from fatigue Janey dragged herself to the door and with the last of her strength banged on it with her fist. She was close to collapse. Then the door opened.

She saw George. He was wearing a long coat and carrying a large searchlight torch.

'Oh,' said Janey, and then she fainted.

Chapter Fifteen

In the cottage, Ross regained consciousness. Switching on the torch he looked around him, dazed, and noticed the mobile phone by his side.

As he tried to retrieve it he winced at the pain in his stomach. He seemed not to realise what had happened and wore a quizzical expression when he moved his hand from his stomach and saw that the cloth that came away with it was covered in blood.

Then it all came back to him, and so did the pain. Nevertheless, he succeeded in retrieving the phone and managed to press the redial button.

Janey was lying in a bed. Daylight filtered through the curtained windows and she fluttered her eyelashes briefly on the way to regaining consciousness.

The first thing she saw was a photograph on the bedside cabinet. It showed the girl, Rosie, sitting atop her pony in best show gear.

Janey reached out with difficulty and tried to touch the pony's nose in the photograph.

Then she was aware of a woman's voice, and her memory returned. There was suddenly fear in her eyes.

'She wakes at last,' announced Margaret, who then saw the fear in Janey's eyes. 'Don't be frightened,' she soothed.

Janey tried to speak but nothing would come out; her mouth was very dry and the swelling from the beating she had taken made any movement difficult.

'You weren't making much sense last night,' continued Margaret. 'It took us a long time to understand what you were saying. You were quite out of it.'

Margaret then busied herself with straightening the bed sheets. 'George was about to come and see how you were coping with the weather in that cottage of yours. He had to turn back when the bulb in his torch went out. 'She paused and patted Janey's hand. 'Still you're here now. Your colour is looking a lot better.'

Then she held Janey's hand. 'The police are here. I'd better call them in. Expect you could do with a nice cup of tea.'

At the mention of the police the fear in Janey's eyes lessened a little. Margaret moved to the door but it was opened from outside and a policeman entered.

'I *thought* I heard talking,' he said.

'I'll leave you alone for a bit.'

'Thanks, Margaret. If you're making tea, I wouldn't mind another.'

Janey tried to sit up.

'Now, Janey,' censured the policeman. 'Can I call you Janey?'

Janey nodded.

'Now, Janey, just take it easy. You've been in the wars, that's plain to see. But the doc says you'll be okay.'

'You've got to help me,' she pleaded, her voice hoarse and crackling. 'And there's a man injured …'

'Steady on. It's all right. Your mouth will be dry after what the doctor gave you. Wait until you get your tea.'

He took out his notebook. 'While we wait, I'll fill you in with what's been happening. Just realise that you are safe - and listen.'

'But George is still out there,' she insisted.

A few miles to the east along the coast and battling through much improved weather at five hundred feet, the helicopter was approaching its destination at a good pace. This didn't appear to be the opinion of one of its two passengers, however. Luke was looking anxiously out of the window of the helicopter. 'Won't this thing go any faster?' he pleaded.

'Janey, listen!' The policeman's tone was firm.

Janey subsided back onto the bed and closed her eyes. Her hands were clenched, holding the bed-clothes tightly.

'We received a call from Mr White, from your mobile phone, and we got the paramedics out to him via land-rover in the early hours.'

Janey's eyes were now wide open, anxious. 'How is he?'

The Policeman looked down at his notebook so Janey couldn't see his expression, which was one of concern. 'He's lost a lot of blood and was quite badly injured. He's stable but they're moving him to a fancy hospital in London.'

'Thank God,' sighed Janey.

The door opened and Margaret entered with a tray. In the background Janey could see George, standing, and looking directly at her, his expression was quizzical.

Margaret smiled and placed the tray on a side table.

Janey looked back towards George and saw he was smiling.

'Drink your tea,' said Margaret. 'You'll feel better.'

Janey wasn't listening. Wild eyed, she pulled the bedclothes up to her chin.

Margaret, her expression showing concern, turned away from Janey and exchanged glances with the policeman.

'Be gentle, Colin,' she told him. 'She's been through a lot.'

Margaret left, shaking her head slightly, and closed the door behind her.

From outside came the sound of an engine.

The policeman had been looking closely at Janey throughout the time Margaret had been bringing in the tea and had seen Janey's reaction to the sight of her husband. 'Oh, I see now,' he said, his intense expression clearing. Then he smiled. 'George didn't attack you and your friend.'

'He didn't? Are you sure?' Her tone was incredulous. 'He…'

The policeman raised a hand to cut her off. 'I can see it must have seemed that way to you but, in fact, the man who attacked you was Ronnie Armitage.'

'Ronnie Armitage,' she repeated, puzzled. Then: 'Mr Armitage? At the Grange?'

'Yes. We found his body at the bottom of the cliffs at first light. They're recovering it now.'

'Mr Armitage. Not George,' she said to herself, testing the logic of the situation. Then, more excitedly she said: 'Of course, he could get access to the cottage with his own key and my sketch in the biscuit tin could have been planted at the Grange to put doubt in my mind about Ross.'

'Come again?'

'Never mind. I'm just realising that Mr Armitage did his best to muddy the waters and deflect suspicion from him.'

The Policeman tried to interrupt.

Janey was having none of it. 'It could have been part of his sick perversion, something to remember the girl by. Perhaps our finding it put the pressure on him to do something about me and Ross because he suspected we'd eventually check with the owner.'

The Policeman looked puzzled.

'The pony knew,' she continued. 'It's so obvious now. He didn't react to Ross clapping his hands at the show. It was seeing Mr Armitage.'

Janey looked at the tea but didn't drink it. Then: 'And he was standing by the first fence.' She looked

174

indignant. 'By God, he cost me the first fence! He cost me a clear round!'

The policeman shook his head. 'Well, I won't pretend to follow all that. You're ahead of me.'

'Armitage, not George,' she said, with evident relief. Her eyes closed again as she took in the significance of this. That she was finally safe.

Then her eyes opened.

'Poor Mrs Armitage.'

The policeman brightened as he recognised something of what she was talking about at last. 'We've already started the investigation. We found some things at the Grange and a box of photographs at the cottage.

'That's the box I'm talking about. The biscuit tin.'

'Right,' he said, and wrote something in his notebook. 'We were as perplexed as you with the deerstalker, but figured he wanted you to believe it was George who was looking through ..'

There was a commotion outside and the door opened. Luke entered, but was talking to someone outside as he did so. 'No, darling,' he said, quietly. 'You stay there. I'll speak to Mummy first.'

'Luke!'

'Janey, darling.'

'Bring Sunny. I need to see Sunny.'

Luke frowned then turned to get Sunny.

Janey looked to the policeman.

'I can do the rest on my own,' he said, taking the hint. 'I'm sure you'd like to be alone.' Then he smiled conspiratorially to Janey, and nodded in the direction of the tea tray. 'I think it is safe to drink the tea now, don't you?'

The policeman moved to the door, acknowledging Luke.

'Colin, is it?' asked Janey.

The Policeman turned round to face Janey.

'Thank you,' she said.

Luke was facing Janey and was unsighted of the policeman, who winked and touched the side of his nose with his finger.

The Policeman left the room.

Luke placed Sunny on the bed and Janey hugged her. 'I've missed you, darling,' she said.

'We've missed you,' said Luke.

Luke reached out to hold Janey's hand. Janey snatched her hand away and turned to smile at a sleepy Sunny.

Margaret pushed a cup of tea towards the policeman. 'They'll be glad of a few minutes alone.'

'What prompted you to go out last night, George?' It was the policeman.

'I'm not sure,' he replied. Then he winced. 'Well, sort of. Maggie said she wondered how the lass was coping with the weather last night.' He shook his head. 'But there was something else. Foreboding I suppose you'd call it.'

George moved to where the torch was sitting on a shelf. He picked it up. 'I got out there...could hardly see a thing, even when I switched this on. The glare from the snow, you see. Then the blasted thing went out. It was all I could do to find my way back.'

George looked at the lamp. 'I found a bulb.'

He switched it on. It was very bright. He moved his head away and shook it, rubbing his eyes with his free hand.

'Like a lighthouse,' said the policeman.

'Anyway,' continued George, 'I was about to go out again when she turned up.' He nodded to the bedroom door. 'She told you about Bracken?'

'Bracken?'

'Our daughter's pony. He's been out and about.'

The policeman face was blank, uncomprehending.

'Bracken brought Miss Holland back. That is, until the pony stumbled and threw her. Miss Holland thinks the pony fell over the cliff. She was rambling a lot during the night but that seems to be what happened.'

The policeman made a face. 'I'm sorry to hear that. I'll investigate, of course.'

Luke was puzzled. Janey looked away. Sunny was almost asleep, curled up in Janey's arms.

'Janey. You're safe now,' he said. 'What's the matter?'

Janey was still looking away. 'I called a number Ross had called. You answered.' She looked directly at Luke. 'You were spying on me!'

'It wasn't like that.'

'You were. You were spying on me. You and Ross. Why?'

Luke looked uncomfortable. 'We want you back, Janey,' he said quietly. 'Sunny and me. We want you back.'

'What are you talking about.?

Luke was suddenly annoyed. 'If you'd just shut up and listen you'll find out!'

Janey flinched and sat back, shocked.

'For the past few years you've been on a tread-mill...'

'We've been through all that. Why were you spying on me?'

'No, more like a war,' he continued, ignoring her question. 'A series of battles between you and whoever your current adversary might be. With Sunny and I collateral damage as usual....'

'This is old stuff. Answer the question.'

Luke put up his hand. 'This is your... what, fourth mini breakdown. Each time you seem to get well and go back into the fray as if nothing is wrong. But there is something wrong. You are less and less the person I married and who Sunny calls Mummy. More a stranger who occasionally comes into our home.'

'We've been over this time and time again,' said Janey, her tone offhand. 'Answer the question.'

Luke went to pick up her hand. She resisted the urge to pull it away and he held it.

'Someone else's home,' he continued. 'You'd forgotten how to live. To have fun. To touch.'

Luke squeezed her hand. Janey responded. She's was crying.

'I went along with you on your other bouts of illness..,' he continued.

Janey was about to remonstrate with him but Luke silenced her with a hard stare.

'Illnesses,' he repeated. 'And kept silent. This time I was going to be more…..proactive. I organised it. I said I would, didn't I?' He leaned forward. 'Janey, I wanted you to learn how to live again.'

'You mean you were prepared to...'

'Lose you? Yes. Whatever it took.' He shrugged. 'Besides, it was no contest. I…we'd already lost you. My plan at least gave us a chance to get you back.'

Janey squeezed his hand and hugged a sleeping Sunny. 'You were prepared to do that.'

Luke remained silent.

Janey looked around her, struggling with her thoughts. 'I don't know if I should tell you this…'.

'Then don't,' said Luke, quickly.

'Ross…. He was injured,' said Janey.

'Will be fine. Don't make this harder than it is.'

'You? Sunny?'

'Want you back. What about you? Do you want us back?

Luke embraced Janey and Sunny. Janey was sobbing.

The helicopter lifted off from the cliff edge in a flurry of snow a hundred yards from George and Margaret. They and the policeman waved as it moved away over the cliffs and began to turn to fly along the coast.

Janey, Luke, and Sunny were sat on the back seat. Janey was holding a flat parcel done up in brown paper.

'Is that your painting?' Luke nodded towards the parcel.

'No. I think someone else has got that. This is something more special.' A faraway look came into Janey's eyes but it was tinged with sadness.

As they gained altitude and proceeded down the coast they looked down and saw a number of people in the garb of emergency workers gathered around a stretcher at the bottom of the cliffs.

Just as she was about to look away again, Janey saw something move from the corner of her eye. It was farther along the cliffs, at a place on the beach from where a long rock platform rose gradually to the cliff top. Along it was running a pony. Her pony.

She drew the others attention to it and started to cry. At the same time she pressed her open palm to the glass as if trying to touch the pony.

Then Janey moved back against the seat and grabbed both Luke and Sunny to her and began kissing them in turn.

Chapter Sixteen

Ross was lying in bed, propped up on the pillows against the sloping metal frame. The only other person in the side-ward was Janey, who was stood by the bed. The mood was strained.

'You've decided?' he asked.

'I'm going back to work tomorrow.'

'That's not what I meant and you know it,' he said, resignedly.

'I know what you meant, but this is difficult. We had a holiday romance. I was ill.'

'Ah-ah, progress. She admits it. I wasn't ill, though. I thought we had something.'

'Oh, we did. But .. but in a way you were your own worst enemy. You brought back all that I had lost. You. The pony. Even the cottage. I finally realised what I've been missing these past few years.

'A victim of my own success. I brought you to your senses and you chose the sensible option.'

'Stop it, please,' implored Janey.

'I'd like to be more gracious but I seem to be having difficulty in that regard.'

'What will you do now?'

'I'm not sure. I gave up the lease on the Grange. The owner is breaking up the property into lots. Two deaths is two too many.'

'I heard.'

'Of course. Luke called in last week,' confirmed Ross. 'I hope he interpreted my surliness as the effects of my physical injuries rather than mental ones. He's got some grand plans for you both.'

'We haven't decided anything yet.'

'No. He told me he was waiting for your decision. Your career will probably get in the way.'

A strained silence followed and lasted a few seconds.

'You really are a psychiatrist? How did you come to be at the Grange?'

'I knew Luke from rugby — we used to play for the same team. I was doing some work in the area, on the death of the girl, and it was easy for me to relocate to the Grange. Anyway, Luke was paying for it.' He smiled a little smile. 'I moved in a week before you arrived.'

Again, silence descended heavily upon the room.

When he spoke again Ross's tone was lighter. 'I'll probably go to Italy,' he decided. 'That's where the bruised hearted go, isn't it.'

'But your work. The murder case and the pictures of the girl.'

Ross was distracted. 'Armitage. That was one *mean* character. They're still digging up stuff on him from over the years. Incidentally, your nightmare...'

'At the Grange?' Janey was surprised.

'I've had time to work out what happened. Armitage got in your room and opened the window. Then he started searching for the incriminating evidence, not realising that I had the biscuit tin which contained it. He thought you were well out of it, but it shows how cool he could be. He just left by the window and...'

'That's what I couldn't understand,' said Janey, suddenly interested.

'Well, the cool bit is that when we all charged into your bedroom and you said the burglar had gone through the window he went over to the window and checked the lock. Except that he was actually locking it. Then he leant on the dresser and shut the drawer, undermining your story in two simple moves. As I say, a cool operator...and a nasty one.'

'He really was at the window outside the cottage all those times, wasn't he?' she asked. 'I thought I was imagining it. But why? What was his motive?'

'Yes, I wondered that, too. Perhaps he wanted to spook you out of the cottage so that he could recover the photos. Then again, perhaps he thought he could sneak in while you were there. It doesn't matter now; it's just a bad dream.'

'Parts of it weren't,' she said, instantly regretting saying it.

Ross did not react and the silence intervened once more until he said, his tone upbeat: 'They tell me this injury will keep me out of circulation for some time.'

'Couldn't you use the time to write up the story, based on the new evidence?'

'All in the public domain now,' he sighed. 'I was hardly in any state to conceal the evidence when they picked me up at the cottage. The police have it all.'

'I'm sorry. And I'm sorry we got involved and…'

'Ah, what the hell. We had something, as you say. Enjoy life Janey, you deserve it,' he said, with an effort. 'And think about me sometime, hmm?'

Janey kissed him on the forehead. 'I will.'

She turned to leave but then turned back.

Ross turned away from her.

'Thank you, Ross, for everything.' A tear rolled down her cheek. She turned blindly for the door and managed to squeeze out into the corridor.

Ross was lying on his side, his back to the door. His eyes were squeezed tight.

As she closed the door she looked up at the name scrawled on the whiteboard: Dr. R. Cardle.

Janey walked purposely along the corridor, dressed for work and carrying a framed package. The PAs were at their desks but Claire rose and intercepted her.

'We thought you would be away longer,' she said.

'It's good to be back,' said Janey brightly. 'I needed to come back. How have things been?'

'Oh. Okay.'

Gerry's door opened and he stepped out.

'Janey, old girl. Glad to have you back,' he said. He nodded towards the package. 'A present for me?'

'Alas, no,' she replied. 'But there may be one in a couple of weeks.'

Janey moved past her PA and opened the door to her office. A man was sitting at her desk.

Janey turned to Gerry with a quizzical expression tinged with a little apprehension.

'I'm sure Gary is only too glad to see you,' said her boss.

Gary stood and reached for a bundle on his desk which he threw onto a pile of bumph. He smiled. 'Welcome back, Janey. With respect, you can keep your job!'

Janey smiled.

Then she began to undo her package. By eye-contact alone Claire, realised Janey wanted to replace the 'Breaking Waves' picture with her package and stepped up to the wall and removed the old painting.

In its place Janey placed a picture of the pony - a blown up version of the picture she had seen at George and Margaret's cottage.

She looked at the picture, straightening it. 'Ah. Thank goodness for horses.'

'We'll give you a bit of time to get your bearings again. We've got a meeting with Gary today some-time.'

Gerry glanced questioningly at Claire.

'Not for another thirty five minutes. Then we've got the HoDs at four. I'm going to need some time to go through your diary, too,' she said.

Janey smiled, weakly. 'Okay,' she said. Then she turned and hid her expression, one of apprehension. 'I look forward to it.'

Gerry, Gary, and Claire left. Janey was alone. She looked up at the picture again. Then she looked around.

'Nothing has changed, really,' she said, reflectively. 'Yes, this will do...for a week or two. Clear up a few loose ends.'

Janey went over to the picture and straightened it again. 'Then? Who knows?

Epilogue

Janey was sat in front of a computer holding a phone. In the background there was the sound of laughter.

She put the phone down and sighed, happy that she had made the life-changing decision that she hoped would prevent a recurrence of her recent problems. She had removed herself from the situation that caused the problem, a much better alternative to treatment and the mumbo-jumbo of psychiatrists, she told herself. Now she was in charge of her life, working from home on a project with much less stress and, it must be admitted, much less money. But here it was also much cheaper to live than in London. Whichever way she looked at it, she told herself, it was the answer, the solution to her problem and she woke up each day thanking Luke for rescuing her from herself.

Even now she was unclear what role Steve had played in Luke's shenanigans. The pressure at the office that she had been feeling before her departure to the cottage was in no small way due to his influence. She was sure now that he had been doing nothing unreasonable at the time; that she had been seeing slights that just were not there. It appeared that Steve had been helpful to Luke and, against her earlier misgivings, was actually on her side throughout her troubles.

The forgetfulness—the dismaying instant loss of memory in the middle of a sentence—had largely disappeared now. It returned even in moments of slight stress but the improvement brought about by her new lifestyle had reduced its impact almost completely.

On the desk stood the small photograph frame containing the list of symptoms signalling a psychotic event, the object Luke had given her all those months ago. She looked at it now, reading the phrase Luke had engineered into the text as two vertical words: 'PASSAGES AFRAID'. It was still a bit too deep for her, but Luke had told her it was the secret to reading the whole thing. His view was that all the obstacles that life puts in front of us are mainly just fears of something or other—most of which have no basis in reality.

'Whatever,' she had responded, dismissively.

Now she looked at the poem in the frame and smiled. She knew what message she would take from it. 'Lest we forget,' she said, aloud, to the empty room.

Doctor Ross Cardle raised himself with difficulty from the chair. He wobbled, a little uncertainly, supporting himself with both hands as he leaned heavily on the desk. His difficulties were only in part due to his injuries, now almost mended. Mostly it was the brandy that was beginning to take its toll and his co-ordination was adversely affected.

On his desk, the laptop computer was displaying the last of his writing. He knew it wasn't good, he'd have to amend it - tomorrow maybe, when he'd sobered up, or much, much, later when he felt a tiny bit better. For now, it was the best he could do.

Bleary eyed, he looked over what he had written: 'Things hadn't been easy following that terrible night in the blizzard, now some four months past. She'd had to make some adjustments to complete the intended therapy begun with her stay at the cottage.

'Chief among these was her belated acceptance that she had a problem. A return to doing the things that had brought Luke and herself together in the first place was another major step in the right direction.

'She had also undergone some more time-lining - where she went back in her memory along the events in her history to located those traumatic events which her mind had worked so hard to shut out, and which were often the precursors to the kind of mental difficulty she had experienced. In this way she had discovered a number of small events which she had forgotten or, rather, her subconscious had hidden from her everyday consciousness. Some were seemingly insignificant taken alone, but they aggregated with others into a set of obstacles that had conspired, with the addition of a stressful job, to bring her to the brink of nervous collapse.

'As already stated, some of the events were seemingly innocuous, an unconscious slight from a valued friend during a period of high stress being one example. Others were more sinister: the rough treatment from a teacher at the tender age of six and only a few years later, being involved in a car crash in which a school friend had died most horrifically. These and other memories, revisited with the benefit of maturity were events that could now be mentally cauterised fully and with impunity. And, what was more important, remove the obstacles to her—and her family's - happiness.

'But it is worth repeating that the most important step had been for her to finally recognise that there was a problem, to convince herself that her self-proclaimed diagnosis of 'only being tired' was just plain wrong. Although it was not part of the plan— and in no way recommended as a treatment regime— this realisation had only come about through the life-threatening events on the night of the blizzard. It had taken such an event to break down her resistance and gain her acceptance of what the problem was: the inflexibility she had built up over many years which, when challenged by a change in the rules in the higher-echelons of her company, had fractured and undermined her entire world. That she had sacrificed all, including her family, to win in the struggle with her career, was the constant driver of her insanity to keep fighting. This, in contrast to what a reasonable person would do: avoid the situation or bend a little to accommodate the stresses involved.

'Luke had tried to get her to understand her problem and failed. Her denial, which she took as strength was, in reality, her weakness and prevented the resolution of her problem. Three times he had tried to convince her of this and failed in each attempt. In so doing, he had watched his marriage, his life, and the happiness of his child heading inexorably down the tubes.

'Breaking such an impasse required strong measures, which is why Luke had decided upon his high-stakes strategy. Faced with Janey's intractable demand to be alone in the back of beyond, his first responsibility had been to ensure her safety and he had achieved that by asking a friend to keep an eye on her. Then he had asked the friend to bring her out of herself. Luke gambled that she would, having been tricked into seeing a little of a better way of life, remember the better days and return to the family he was striving to keep together. The gamble, despite the pain and suffering which had been shared out among a number of people, appeared to have succeeded.'

Ross felt for the mouse and, in so doing, pushed the glass off the desk to crash into a thousand pieces on the tiled floor. Ignoring the mess he moved the mouse and clicked on shutdown.

Then he turned to look at the diploma on the wall, the fragments of glass crackling beneath his feet. The diploma was his *raison d'être*, his medical qualification, the instrument that drove him on.

'What's the point?' he asked himself, sadly. 'Who heals the physician?' Then he shrugged. 'Of course,' he announced, to the empty room, 'Physician heal thyself!'

In his slightly inebriated state he appeared to find this very amusing for he laughed aloud. But it wasn't a pleasant laugh and his expression was not humorous.

'Janey,' he breathed, quietly, and his eye automatically sought out the picture on the wall, 'Breaking Waves.'

Then he turned and reached again for the brandy bottle and a fresh glass.

Janey pressed a button on the computer keyboard and the screen went blank. 'That'll do it for today,' she said, cheerfully.

Then she rose and walked through the open french windows and into the warm sunlight on the terrace. As she approached the others her expression was reflective. At one point she paused and turned around to look back at the Grange, not knowing why she did so. Fleetingly, she imagined she saw Ross wave from the window. She had to stop herself from waving back. Then she turned around and walked towards the others. She was happy, she decided.

In front of her, Luke was fussing around the pony, atop which was sat Sunny.

Janey joined them. They were all laughing. Even the pony seemed to be in a good mood. Then something about Bracken made her stop in her tracks and she looked him in the eye.

He winked!

THE END

www.ingramcontent.com/pod-product-compliance
Lightning Source LLC
Chambersburg PA
CBHW060938180626
46817CB00004B/1604